"*Tate, please don't stop,*"

she pleaded. "I want you to love me."

"But we need to talk, remember? We need to think about what we want."

"I know what I want. I want to feel you inside me. I—I've never felt that before, and I want it to be with you."

A thrill of pleasure soared through Tate, then turned to doubt. After all, she still thought they were unsuitable. So did he, for that matter. Nothing had happened to change that, and making love would only confuse matters.

She gazed up at him, and there was a mute appeal in her eyes, an appeal it was taking every ounce of willpower he possessed to deny.

"Please," she whispered. "Please..."

Dear Reader,

Welcome to Silhouette! Our goal is to give you hours of unbeatable reading pleasure, and we hope you'll enjoy each month's six new Silhouette Desires. These sensual, provocative love stories are both believable and compelling—sometimes they're poignant, sometimes humorous, but always enjoyable.

Indulge yourself. Experience all the passion and excitement of falling in love along with our heroine as she meets the irresistible man of her dreams and together they overcome all obstacles in the path to a happy ending.

If this is your first Desire, I hope it'll be the first of many. If you're already a Silhouette Desire reader, thanks for your support! Look for some of your favorite authors in the coming months: Stephanie James, Diana Palmer, Dixie Browning, Ann Major and Doreen Owens Malek, to name just a few.

Happy reading!

Isabel Swift
Senior Editor

SDRL-7/85

SHERRYL WOODS
Yesterday's Love

Silhouette Desire

Published by Silhouette Books New York

America's Publisher of Contemporary Romance

SILHOUETTE BOOKS
300 East 42nd St., New York, N.Y. 10017

ISBN: 0-373-05329-0

First Silhouette Books printing January 1987

All the characters in this book are fictitious. Any
resemblance to actual persons, living or dead, is
purely coincidental.

America's Publisher of Contemporary Romance

Printed in the U.S.A.

Books by Sherryl Woods

Silhouette Desire

Not at Eight, Darling #309
Yesterday's Love #329

SHERRYL WOODS

lives by the ocean, which provides daily inspiration for the romance in her soul. Her years as a television critic taught her about steamy plots and humor. Her years as a travel editor took her to exotic locations. Her years as a crummy weekend tennis player taught her to stick with what she enjoyed most: writing. What better way to combine all that than by writing romantic stories about wonderful heroines, sensitive heroes and enchanting locations.

For Nancy, whose rare combination of zaniness and practicality, make her a very special friend and for Andy, who's brought her happiness and romance.

One

Tears streaming down her pale cheeks, Victoria flipped off the television by remote control and reached blindly for the box of tissues beside her on the huge brass bed. When her groping fingers met the empty slot, she muttered a soft expletive, tossed the useless container across the room and wiped away the tears with the back of her hand. *Now, Voyager* always did this to her.

"You'd think by now I'd be prepared, wouldn't you?" she said to the fluffy gray cat that was purring contentedly in her lap. How many times had she sobbed as a resigned Bette Davis pleaded with Paul Henried not to ask for the moon, when they already had the stars? Surely more than a dozen.

Of course, it wasn't just this movie that affected her that way, she noted ruefully. She'd cried through everything from *Jane Eyre* and *Camille* to *Terms of Endearment*. She'd even been known to sniffle a little when two obviously long lost lovers were reunited in a shampoo commercial.

Being a sentimental, hopeless romantic in a world of hardened cynics sometimes seemed to be a wretched curse. She recalled with more than a little dismay the number of times her embarrassed dates had exited a movie joking that they might be able to buy her diamonds, but they doubted they could afford to keep her supplied with Kleenex. Well, to hell with the emotionally uptight men of the world, she thought darkly. They'll all probably wind up with much deserved ulcers.

Climbing out of bed, she ignored Lancelot's outraged cry of protest at being displaced from his comfortable spot in her lap. After she pulled on the long, old-fashioned skirt and scoop-necked blouse she'd found during her last secondhand store excursion, she wandered barefoot into the kitchen. The fragrant scent of lilacs and freshly mowed grass was drifting in with the spring breeze that ruffled the curtains on the open windows. This was her favorite room in the decrepit old farmhouse she'd bought and begun remodeling bit by bit the previous year. Her parents had nicknamed her home Victoria's Folly, but once they'd seen what she'd accomplished with the kitchen, even they had to admit there was hope for the place.

Like the rest of the house, the kitchen had wide-plank hardwood floors, but in here she had stripped away layers of paint and wax and had polished the wood to a soft gleam. The huge windows, cleansed of the thick grime that had accumulated during years of neglect, now let in so much light that the room seemed bright even on the grayest Ohio winter day. She had scoured the once disreputable looking white tile countertops until they sparkled. The crumbling walls had been patched and painted a cheerful yellow, against which she had hung shiny copper pots and pans. She had refinished the round oak table and chairs in the middle of the room herself. And in the center of the table stood an antique blue-and-white water pitcher filled with daffodils from her garden.

"Okay, old guy, what shall we do about lunch?" she asked the cat who was now staring at her patiently from the sun-warmed windowsill. "Tuna? Liver? Chicken?" She waited for a responding meow. There was none. "You're not helping, Lancelot." She opened a can of the liver he seemed to love, wrinkled her nose in disgust and put it in his dish.

"You have no taste, cat," she said, as he arched haughtily and then made his way slowly to the dish of food she'd placed on the floor.

While Lancelot methodically devoured the liver, Victoria searched in the back of the huge, walk-in pantry for her picnic basket. The day was too incredibly gorgeous to waste one more minute of it indoors. She filled the wicker basket with chunks of Gouda and cheddar cheese, two freshly baked poppy seed rolls she'd bought at the bakery on her way home from her antique shop the previous afternoon, a bottle of chilled mineral water and a container of strawberries.

She tossed a dog-eared volume of Elizabeth Barrett Browning's poetry in on top, took her floppy, wide-brimmed straw hat from the peg by the back door and set out across the rolling field behind the house. Lancelot, through with his meal, trailed at her heels sniffing hopefully amid the buttercups for the scent of a field mouse.

When she reached the huge, ancient oak tree that shaded the back corner of her property, she spread out her red-checked tablecloth and settled down for her picnic, barely noticing the taste of the food as she lost herself in the sad, poetic spell Browning had woven.

How do I love thee? Let me count the ways
I love thee to the depth and breadth and height
My soul can reach, when feeling out of sight
For the ends of Being and ideal Grace.

For the second time that day, she felt misty-eyed. Would she ever love someone this much, she wondered despondently. Nothing in her twenty-eight years indicated that she had the potential for such deep emotion. Certainly none of the men she'd met up until now had ever stirred a passionate response from her. Their kisses, their practiced touches had been mildly enjoyable, but nothing more. Maybe she was doomed to a life of lukewarm relationships. The thought was incredibly depressing, especially for someone who truly believed it was love that made the world go around.

Sighing heavily, she glanced up from the sonnet she'd been reading just in time to see Lancelot spring into the tree above her with surprising agility for a cat his size and age.

"Lancelot, no!" she shouted futilely, as he landed on a limb high above her head. "Lancelot, you know you're terrified of heights. Now what are you going to do?"

She shook her head as the cat uttered a pathetic meow.

"You got yourself up there," she reminded him unsympathetically. "Now get yourself down."

Lancelot seemed to shiver, then meowed again more loudly. He sounded pitiful, far too pitiful to ignore.

"Okay. Okay. I'm coming," she said resignedly, dropping her book onto the tablecloth and hiking up her skirt. She shinnied up the tree in the awkward, uneasy manner of someone who'd done this often in the past but never grown accustomed to it. To be perfectly truthful, she wasn't one bit fonder of heights than Lancelot was. To top it off, the minute she got near him, the cat backed out of her reach. "Lancelot, how can I rescue you if you keep moving away from me?"

She tested the strength of the limb and shifted until her body rested along the length of it. Stretching as far as she could, she tried again to grab the cat, whose cries had grown more shrill. Taking a deep breath, Victoria crept another few inches. "Here, Lancelot. Come on, fellow," she whispered encouragingly, just as she heard the branch creak and felt it waver beneath her. The tremor shook her confidence and her patience. "Lancelot, get over here right this minute!"

The cat didn't budge, but the limb dipped precariously and Victoria glanced nervously down at the ground. It seemed much farther away than she'd remembered. Clinging tightly to the branch while she tried to decide whether to risk a retreat or spend the next fifty years of her life right here living on bark, acorns and oak leaves, she looked off in the distance and spotted the welcome sight of someone heading in her direction.

With his determined, long-legged stride and squared jaw, the unfamiliar man looked like someone with a definite and probably unpleasant mission. Even from this distance and this crazy, sort of upside-down angle, she could tell he was physically impressive. His broad shoulders, beneath a pale blue shirt that was shadowed with perspiration, were obviously well formed and muscular. The tan slacks were slung low on slim hips, the fit emphasizing the curve of his thighs, the length of his powerful legs. His tie was askew, and he was carrying a tan jacket slung over his shoulder. He was definitely not dressed like someone who'd planned to go for a stroll in the country.

She shaded her eyes and squinted into the sun, studying what she could make out of the chiseled features of his face and the dark brown hair that needed cutting. Her breath caught in her throat.

"Good Lord, if I'm dreaming, don't let me wake up," she murmured under her breath as he approached, his expression growing puzzled as he noted the tablecloth, the picnic basket and the book.

"Hi," she said cheerfully, trying to keep a nervous tremor out of her voice. The last crack of the limb had tilted it until her head seemed nearly perpendicular to the blanket. As soft as the ground had seemed when she'd been sitting on it, she had no particular desire to land on it headfirst and test its resiliency.

Startled by the husky, whispered greeting, Tate McAndrews looked around for the person whose entrancing voice had seemed to come to him from the heavens.

"Up here."

He gazed up and stared into a pair of very wide, very blue eyes that glinted with suppressed laughter. His heart took an unexpected lurch.

"Hi, yourself," he said, his irritation at the rotten way the day had gone suddenly vanishing in the presence of such unabashed, impish humor. Perhaps this wild-goose chase he'd been sent on would have an unexpected dividend after all. "Do you always perch in trees after lunch?"

"Hardly," she said with a grimace that wrinkled her pert nose in a delightful way. "By the way, my name's Victoria Marshall and I'm very glad to see you. I seem to have gotten myself into a bit of a predicament."

Tate groaned and a pained expression replaced the quirk of amusement that had played about his lips. So much for any thoughts of pleasant diversions. His wild-goose chase had ended. "I should have known," he muttered.

"Is something wrong?"

He shook his head. "No. In fact, I was looking for you."

"You were? Do I know you?"

"Not yet, but you will," he mumbled ominously. "I'm Tate McAndrews. Internal Revenue Service."

Usually people panicked at the mere mention of the IRS, but Tate had to give Victoria Marshall credit. She didn't even flinch.

"Oh, that's nice," she said brightly and with such sincerity that Tate had to believe she had no idea what he was doing here. "But do you suppose you could help me get down before we continue this conversation? My head is beginning to spin."

"What are you doing up there in the first place?"

"Lancelot saw a squirrel."

"Lancelot? A squirrel?" He felt strangely light-headed, as though he were rapidly losing the capability of rational thought. It was either this unseasonably warm weather or this perky woman he'd discovered hanging upside down in a tree with her skirt hitched up in a decidedly provocative way. He preferred to think it was the weather.

"Lancelot is my cat. He's twelve and he mostly just lazes around now, but a squirrel will get to him every time."

"I see." Actually Tate didn't see at all. But he was beginning to understand that this assignment that Pete Harrison had foisted off on him was not going to be quite as easy and straightforward as he'd anticipated. He berated himself for not guessing that any woman who would demand that the IRS send her a refund for $15,593.12 more than she had paid in taxes was not exactly your run-of-the-mill evader. She was a kook. Everything that had happened in the last few minutes only confirmed the fact. She might be very attractive in an offbeat sort of way, but she was a kook nonetheless.

Still, she was also up in the tree, and he couldn't wrap up this absurd business about the refund until she came down. It would probably be best if she didn't do it headfirst and shake any more of her screws loose.

"Let go of the branch," he suggested.

"Are you crazy?" she replied in a horrified, hushed whisper, her eyes widening as the branch tipped a bit more. "I'm twelve feet off the ground. I'll break every bone in my body."

"Don't worry. I'm going to catch you."

"Then I'll break every bone in your body."

"I'll take my chances," he retorted. "Come on. Just let go and drop down."

"But what about Lancelot?"

"I don't think you need to worry about him," Tate replied dryly.

Victoria followed his gaze and saw that the traitorous cat was sitting serenely in the middle of the tablecloth eating the last of the Gouda cheese. "Lancelot, how could you?" she muttered.

"You might as well jump."

Sighing nervously, Victoria swung her legs around, allowing them to dangle as she clung tightly to the increasingly unsteady branch. She glanced down uneasily into Tate McAndrews's upturned face. "Are you sure about this?"

"I'm sure."

"Okay," she said, closing her eyes as she let go. There was no point in looking. It was up to Tate McAndrews to make good on his promise to catch her.

She tried to think of herself as weightless, a butterfly floating on air, but it wasn't working. She felt as though she were plummeting like a rock. Her heart thudded against her ribs in anticipation of the crash landing that would leave them both in a tangle of broken bones.

Suddenly, just when she was sure it was too late, that she'd only imagined someone was going to save her from cracking her skull, she felt strong arms break her fall. As the breath whooshed out of her, her own arms instinctively circled Tate's shoulders. She hung on for dear life.

"You can open your eyes now," he said, his husky, laughter-filled voice a whisper of disturbing warmth against her flushed cheek.

Victoria wasn't sure she wanted to if it meant he would put her down. She was surprised to discover that she rather liked his tangy male scent, the rippling strength of his arms, the warmth that radiated through his clothes. He appealed to so many of her senses: touch, smell and—most definitely she decided, peeking at his chiseled profile—sight. The man was even more gorgeous than he'd appeared from her perch in the tree. Definitely romantic hero material, she thought, sighing unconsciously.

Tate heard the sigh and realized with a sense of shock that he was apparently having a very similar reaction. It was a reaction that was both unexpected and totally inappropriate. Ten years with IRS had hardened him, made him cynical about human nature in general and especially about the type of people who tried to bilk the government. They were thieves, and it was his job to catch them and see that they paid. Nothing more, nothing less. It was all very business-like, very impersonal. Sometimes he spent months on a case, shadowing a subject's every move, getting to know the most intimate secrets of his or her life, but never before had he responded to one of them on a personal level.

Then again, he had to admit that none of his previous subjects had ever looked like Victoria Marshall. He lowered her gently to the checked tablecloth, then sat down beside her, unable to shift his gaze away. She was like no woman he had ever seen, except, perhaps, in a Renoir painting. She was wearing a long, ruffled cotton skirt in a bright shade of pink that made her seem daringly oblivious to the long red hair that framed her face in a profusion of untamed, golden-highlighted curls. Though those incredibly blue eyes met his gaze with an appealing, interested expression, she was fiddling nervously with a floppy, white straw hat. Her off-the-shoulder white blouse revealed an extraordinary amount of creamy flesh, he noted breathlessly before glancing quickly away only to encounter the enticing sight of her slender, bare feet peeking from beneath the folds of her skirt.

He drew a deep, shuddering breath. This wouldn't do at all. Obviously, Victoria Marshall was smarter than he'd thought. She was probably deliberately trying to appeal to him, to seduce him so that he'd forget all about the little matter of her bizarre tax return. She wouldn't be the first woman to try that. True, most of them were considerably more worldly than she seemed to be, but perhaps this wide-eyed innocence was all an act.

Victoria watched the play of expressions on Tate's face and wondered about them. Warmth. Anger. Determination. She had the feeling that he'd just made a decision about something or someone. Was it her? She didn't want to think so, because his brown eyes were glittering now with a cold hardness that she found almost frightening in its dark intensity.

"Did you bring my check?" she asked hopefully.

He shook his head. "Sorry. The IRS doesn't underwrite bad business debts. Why haven't you answered any of our letters?"

Victoria was puzzled. "I haven't seen any letters." She brightened. "Of course there is a stack of mail on the desk in the shop. They must be there. What were they about?"

"We're auditing you. You were supposed to report with all your records."

"Oh, dear. When?"

"Last week."

"Oh, dear," she repeated contritely. "Would you like some cheese?"

"What?"

"I asked if you would like some cheese," she explained patiently, holding out a chunk of the cheddar that Lancelot hadn't discovered during his raid on the picnic basket. "It's very good."

"Sure. Thanks. About the audit—"

"Couldn't we talk about that later?"

"Look, Ms. Marshall—"

"Call me Victoria."

Tate closed his eyes. His head was beginning to reel again. "Victoria. I drove all the way up here from Cincinnati to straighten out your tax problems. I don't have time to sit under a tree and eat cheese and make small talk with you." She blinked at him rapidly and his determination wavered.

"Much as I might like to," he added to soften the harsh effect of his very firm words. She'd looked as though she might cry and he couldn't stand that. He had come here to find out how much she'd been holding out on the government, not to make her cry.

"But I don't have any tax problems," she insisted stoutly. "I've always sent my return in right on time."

She hesitated, her very kissable pink lips pursed thoughtfully. "At least I think I have. I'm not sure. Paperwork is so boring, don't you think? Anyway, I'm almost certain that I haven't missed a single deadline. I make it a point to put a big red circle around April 15 on my calendar so I won't forget."

"But you asked for a refund of money you'd never paid."

She regarded him indignantly. "How can you say that? I've paid year after year. This last year, when I opened my shop, I lost more money than I earned."

Tate, to his dismay, was beginning to follow her logic. That scared the life out of him. Unleashed on an unsuspecting world, this woman would be dangerous. Beautiful, but kooky as they come. "So you figured the government should reimburse you out of funds you'd previously paid?"

Her eyes sparkled, and she gave him a smile that could light up a skyscraper. "Exactly."

"It doesn't work that way."

"It doesn't?"

"I'm afraid not."

Her smile wavered. "Oh. Well, I guess I'll get by. Business has been picking up lately. Now that it's spring more people seem to go for drives in the country. Most of them can't resist browsing through antiques."

"Do they buy anything?"

She shrugged. "Sometimes. More often than not, they drink a cup of coffee, chat awhile and then go on. That's part of the fun of owning an antique shop...meeting new people."

"You give your customers coffee?"

The look she gave him was withering. "Usually I have a homemade cake, too," she said defensively. "Yesterday I had apple pie, but the crust was soggy. I haven't quite mastered pie crusts yet. I'm not sure what the problem is. Maybe the shortening."

Tate shook his head. He'd obviously been dealing with powerful, cold-blooded corporations too long. He was not prepared to deal with someone who spent more money most days feeding her customers than she took in and then worried about the quality of her cooking on top of it.

"Do you suppose we could take a look at your records?" he said, suddenly impatient to get this over with. He was getting some very strange feelings from this woman and, unfortunately, most of them were very unprofessional. Right now she was looking at him with wide, cornflower-blue eyes filled with hurt, as though he'd rejected her or worse. His pulse rate quickened, and he had the oddest desire to comfort her, to hold her and tell her he'd take care of everything. He drew in a ragged breath and reminded himself sternly that IRS agents, especially those with his reputation for tough, relentless questioning, did not comfort individuals they were about to audit.

"Of course," Victoria replied stiffly. Her first impression obviously had been correct: this man did have a mission, and it seemed he wasn't the type to be dissuaded from pursuing it. It was such a waste, too, she thought with a sigh. With his dashing good looks and trim build, he'd seemed exactly the sort of man she'd been waiting all her life to meet, the type who'd sweep a woman off her feet in the very best romantic tradition. Instead, he seemed to have the soul of a stuffy realist. He was going to wind up with ulcers by the time he hit forty, just like the rest of them.

Disillusioned and disappointed at having to abandon her fantasy so quickly, she gathered up the remnants of her picnic, perched her hat on top of her head and took off across the field, her long skirt billowing in the breeze. She didn't wait to see if Tate McAndrews followed. She knew instinctively that he wasn't about to let her out of his sight. He apparently thought she was some sort of criminal. She huffed indignantly at the very idea. A criminal indeed! Well, he could look at her records, such as they were, from now until doomsday, and he wouldn't find anything incriminating. Once he'd finished, he could apologize and go on his way.

She glanced over her shoulder and caught the frown on his face, the hard, no-nonsense line of his jaw. On second thought, he probably wouldn't apologize.

When they reached the house, Victoria opened the kitchen door and stood aside to allow Tate to enter.

"Why don't you have a seat? I'll get the papers and bring them in here," she suggested. "There's lemonade in the fridge, if you'd like some."

Lemonade? The corners of Tate's mouth tilted up as he watched her disappear into the main part of the house, the long skirt adding a subtle emphasis to the naturally provocative sway of her hips. He couldn't recall the last time anyone had offered him lemonade. Most of the women he knew had a Scotch on the rocks waiting for him when he walked in the door. He picked up two tall glasses from the counter by the sink, went to the refrigerator and filled them with ice. He found the huge pitcher of fresh-squeezed lemonade and poured them each a glass. He took a long, thirst-quenching swallow of the sweet-tart drink. It was perfect after that damnably hot trek through the field. He'd forgotten how good this stuff was. Maybe he was getting a little too jaded after all.

He sat on one of the high-backed chairs, tilted it on two legs and surveyed the room. It had a cheerful, homey feel to it. It was nothing like the pretentious glass and high-tech kitchens he was used to. In fact, he had a feeling Victoria Marshall had never heard of a food processor, much less used one. She'd probably squeezed every one of the lemons for this lemonade with her own hands. The thought proved disturbingly intriguing.

"Slow down, McAndrews. This woman is strictly off-limits," he muttered aloud. Not only was Victoria Marshall the subject of an official IRS investigation, she was totally inappropriate for him. He liked his women sophisticated, fashionable and, most of all, uncommitted. From what he'd seen of Victoria she was about as worldly as a cloistered nun. As for her fashion sense, it would have been fine about one hundred years ago. And, worst of all, she was definitely the type of woman who needed commitments. She'd been reading *Sonnets from the Portuguese*, for crying out loud.

But she was gorgeous. Fragile. Like the lovely old porcelain doll he remembered his mother keeping in a place of honor in her bedroom. That doll had been his great-grandmother's and would be passed along to his daughter if, as his mother reminded him frequently, he would only have the good sense to marry and settle down. He was suddenly struck by the fact that his mother probably would approve thoroughly of someone like Victoria.

"Uh-uh," he muttered emphatically, irritated at the direction his thoughts had taken. He'd better get this over with now before he did something absolutely ridiculous and totally out of character, such as asking Victoria Marshall for a date. His mother might cheer, but Pete Harrison would have his hide for that breach of ethics.

"Where the hell is she?" he groused, lowering the chair to all four sturdy legs with a thud and stalking out of the kitchen. As he went from room to empty room looking for her, his dismay grew. How could she live like this? The place was a shambles. No wonder she'd left him in the kitchen. The wallpaper in the rest of the downstairs was peeling, the floors were warped and weathered, as though they'd spent weeks under floodwaters, and there wasn't a stick of furniture in any of the rooms, unless you counted the old Victorian sofa which had stuffing popping out through holes in the upholstery. It looked as though it would be painfully uncomfortable under the best of repair.

"Victoria!"

"I'll be right down. I'm just trying to get everything together."

"I'll come up."

"Don't do that," she shouted back and he sensed an odd urgency in her voice. "The stairs—"

But before she could finish the warning, Tate had already reached the third step. As soon as he put his weight on it, he felt the stair wobble and heard the wood crack. His ankle twisted painfully and he fell backward, landing with a thud. The crash echoed throughout the house, followed by an explosion of exceptionally colorful curses as Tate lay on the floor, his ankle throbbing, his ego even more bruised than his body.

"Damn Pete Harrison and his so-called breeze of a case!" he growled ominously, completely undone by the emotional and physical shake-up of his life ever since he'd found Victoria Marshall in that damned tree. "I have a feeling I'd be in less danger checking out the head of the mob."

Two

Upstairs, Victoria listened to the cacophony of explosive sounds and winced. Obviously, her incomplete warning had been far too little, too late. Cautiously, she poked her head out the door of her makeshift office-storeroom and peered down into Tate McAndrews's scowling face.

"Are you okay?"

He was getting gingerly to his feet, testing his ankle. "Nothing's broken, if that's what you mean."

"I'm sorry. I tried to warn you."

"So you did," he admitted dryly. "How can you live like this?"

"Like what?" she asked, honestly puzzled by the question. She loved this old house and she'd never been happier anywhere else. It was exactly the sort of home she'd always dreamed of owning, a place with character, with all sorts of interesting nooks and crannies. It would be a terrific place for hide-and-seek.

"This place is falling apart."

She looked at the wobbly stairs, the tattered wallpaper and the dangling light bulb that Tate could see from the downstairs hall. Even she had to admit it didn't give the very best impression of the house. "You have to think in terms of potential," she suggested.

"Potential?"

"Like the kitchen," she explained, deciding that he needed concrete images. Men like Tate McAndrews always did. They seemed to have trouble dealing with the abstractions, with feelings and moods and ambiance.

"You mean the kitchen looked as bad as this?"

"Worse," she admitted. "It was my third project. It turned out rather well, don't you think?"

"You did the kitchen yourself?"

She wasn't sure whether she should be pleased or insulted by his incredulous tone. She decided to remain neutral. "You've seen my tax return. Does it look like I could afford to hire somebody?"

"I guess not."

"Well, then. Of course, if I'd gotten that refund...." Her voice trailed off forlornly.

"Forget it," he advised. "You said the kitchen was your third project. What were the others?"

"The bedroom and bathroom."

Despite himself, Tate was intrigued. Knowing he was going to hate himself later for allowing yet another distraction to keep him from wrapping up this audit and escaping to the relative safety of Cincinnati, he asked, "May I see?"

"Are you sure you want to risk the stairs?"

"Just tell me what the secret is."

"I've fixed every other one," she explained brightly, as though that were a perfectly sensible thing to do.

He looked down and saw what should have been obvious to him in the first place: every second step was made of new wood, polished and solid looking. The ones in-between were broken planks that looked no better than the floors he'd seen in the downstairs rooms. The third one was splintered where his weight had been too much for the dry-rotted wood.

"I should have guessed," he said, taking giant-sized steps to join her. "Lead on. You can warn me where the booby traps are."

"Careful," she whispered conspiratorially. "You'll hurt its feelings."

"Houses don't have feelings."

"Of course they do. They have feelings and personalities all their own."

"This one's obviously split," he murmured.

"What?"

"You know...a split personality. Repaired in some parts. Disastrous in others."

"Very funny."

"I thought it was."

"You would. You obviously have a cruel streak."

"I'll admit I'm not quite as tolerant as you appear to be," he retorted, giving her a grin that shattered her indignation into a thousand pieces. Victoria found herself smiling back at him helplessly.

"Do you want to see the rest or not?" she asked softly, her flashing blue eyes more challenging than her words. A flicker of desire had flared to life in Tate's eyes and Victoria felt a matching tremor of excitement so intense it startled her. So, she thought, this was what the fuss was all about. One minute you're leading a perfectly ordinary, placid existence, and the next minute some thoroughly impossible, sexy man turns up and turns your insides into warm honey. The sensation was both thrilling and frightening.

"Oh, I want," he replied in a low voice, his gaze drifting down over her slender neck and bare shoulders before halting in apparent fascination at the swell of her breasts. There was no doubt in her mind that he wasn't referring to a tour of the house. Victoria suddenly realized with a flush of embarrassment that her nipples were clearly visible beneath the light cotton of her blouse. Worse than that, they seemed to be responding merely to the appreciative warmth of his examination, swelling to an aching tautness. She suddenly felt claustrophobic and had the strangest desire to run. At the same time, she wanted very much to stay right here and see exactly what Tate McAndrews had in mind and whether he meant to follow through on that dangerous glint she thought she'd read in his eyes.

Almost hesitantly, he reached toward her and her heart thundered in anticipation, while her head seemed to be shouting to her to get a grip on herself. Sighing regretfully, she decided that just this once she'd better listen to her head. Before Tate's fingers could touch her cheek, she whirled neatly around and stepped away from him.

"This is the bathroom," she said briskly, determined to keep the shakiness she felt from her voice. Just because Tate McAndrews was the sexiest creature she'd seen since her last viewing of Clark Gable in *Gone With the Wind*, that was no reason for her to go all wobbly and woolly-headed. The man was here to audit her, after all. It wasn't as though he'd asked her for a date. He'd only looked at her as though he'd wanted to...what? To kiss her senseless? And that was what had made her go weak in the knees. It was not a good way to begin a business relationship with an IRS agent, not unless you planned to follow through, which she most certainly did not.

With determinedly cool detachment she showed him the bathroom with its lovely old tiled walls and floor, its huge tub and the circular leaded window that let in shattered streams of bright sun during the day and soft moonlight at night. When they reached her bedroom, her composure slipped a little as she wondered idly what it would be like to have this virile man sharing her huge brass bed, the colorful, handmade quilt tossed anxiously aside in a tangled heap as a desperate, urgent passion made them oblivious to anything except each other. The prospect sent a disturbing shiver racing down her spine, and she blushed and turned away, avoiding his speculative gaze.

"Very nice," he murmured softly, and for one very disconcerting minute she wasn't sure whether he was talking about the bedroom or whether he had read her mind. The possibility that he, too, was looking at that bed and wondering who-knew-what unnerved her. She turned back to study him, a quizzical expression on her face, but he was looking innocently around the room.

"How long do you suppose it's going to take you to do the rest of the house?" he asked with nothing more than casual interest. Victoria wasn't sure whether to feel relieved or disappointed.

"At the rate I'm going, it should be finished by the twenty-first century," she admitted bleakly.

Her response seemed to make him angry for some reason. "You can't go on living like this."

"Of course I can," she retorted. "What's wrong with the way I live?"

"It's not safe."

"It's perfectly safe. Just because the wallpaper is peeling doesn't mean the house will fall down."

"I'm not so sure."

"Well, I am."

"Okay. Okay," Tate said resignedly. Obviously, there was no point in arguing. Besides, it was definitely none of his business how she lived . . . unless, of course, it happened to be beyond her reported means. From what he'd seen today, that was hardly likely.

"Where are those records you came up here to get?" he asked. "I think we'd better go over them and finish this up."

"They're in here," she said, walking down the hall to the door she'd pulled shut as he came up the stairs. "Why don't you go back down to the kitchen and wait for me?"

"Why? Do you have something to hide?" he asked, his highly trained and very suspicious mind instinctively surging into action.

She glared at him. "Of course not. It's just that I'm not sure you are ready for this."

"Ready for what? The room can't be in any worse shape than some of the others I've already seen. I think my system had become immune to the shock."

"It's not the room I'm concerned about."

"What then?"

"I have a feeling you have an orderly mind."

"I do. What does that have to do with anything?"

"My records aren't..." She hesitated. "... Well, they aren't exactly... orderly."

"What are they exactly?"

Victoria sighed and opened the door. "See for yourself."

Tate stepped into the room and immediately his eyes flew open, his eyebrows shooting up in horrified disbelief.

"Holy...!" His voice trailed off, and he stood there, seemingly unable to complete the thought. It was the cry of a wounded man and, for a fraction of a second, Victoria almost felt sorry for him.

"Maybe it would be better if you went back to the kitchen," she repeated in a consoling tone, pulling on his arm. "Have some more lemonade. I'll get what you need and bring it down."

"How? It would take an entire office of accountants to bring order to this... this chaos," he said weakly. He still seemed to be suffering from some sort of professional shock.

"It will only take me a little while," Victoria reassured him. "I know exactly where everything is."

He shook his head disbelievingly. "You couldn't possibly."

"Of course I do. I have a system."

He eyed her wonderingly. "This I have to see," he said, plucking a stack of old magazines off of the room's only chair and settling down to watch. "If you can locate the records you need for last year's tax return, I will buy you dinner in the most expensive restaurant in Cincinnati."

It seemed like a reasonable challenge, though Victoria wasn't at all sure it would be wise to spend an evening in the company of Tate McAndrews. Without even trying, he'd already stirred up all sorts of desires that only this afternoon she'd despaired of ever feeling. What on earth would happen over an intimate dinner? She'd probably fall head over heals in love with the man, and he'd go blithely along to his next audit. It was not a comforting prospect.

Still, she couldn't very well lose the bet on purpose. She had to prove to him that while her system of accounting might be a bit unorthodox by his standards, it was as effective as ledgers and computerized spread sheets.

"Okay, Mr. McAndrews, you're on," she replied determinedly. "How long do I have?"

Tate grinned at her complacently. "Oh, I think I can afford to be lenient. Take as long as you like."

"You really don't think I can do this, do you?"

"No."

"You haven't said what happens if I lose."

"You hire an accountant and get your finances straightened out."

"My finances are fine, thank you. I've never missed a mortgage payment. My electricity's never been turned off. And I don't even own a credit card." She absolutely refused to tell him that she'd lost them and never gotten around to obtaining replacements.

"Thank God," he murmured fervently under his breath.

She regarded him indignantly. "Are you insulting me?"

"Heaven forbid!"

"Then why did you say that?"

"Let's just say that individuals more organized than you seem to have gotten themselves in way over their heads by haphazardly buying with plastic."

To be perfectly truthful, that was exactly why Victoria had decided not to replace the credit cards. It wasn't that she'd overspent. It was that she had this silly habit of misplacing the bills so that she never knew whether they'd been paid or not. By buying with cash she was relatively certain that she, not the credit card company, owned her possessions.

She did not, however, intend to stand here and discuss the relative merits of plastic money with Tate McAndrews. Not when he'd just bet her that she couldn't turn over the receipts she needed to back up her tax return. Taking a deep breath, she surveyed the room and went to work, picking up, studying and then discarding stacks of paper that had been stashed in boxes and bags of every size and shape. Every so often, she triumphantly dumped something new in

Tate's lap or at his feet, gloating at his increasingly bemused expression.

"There," she said at last, standing in front of him with her hands on her hips. "I think that's everything." It had taken her exactly twenty minutes.

Tate looked at the four shoeboxes, two bulging shopping bags, three manila envelopes and one beat-up purse that she'd deposited with him. "This is it?" he said skeptically. "Price Waterhouse would be impressed."

"Don't be sarcastic."

"Sorry. What exactly do I have here?"

"These two boxes have the receipts for everything I bought for the shop last year. These two are all the bills for fixing it up, the mortgage payments on the shop and so on."

"The shopping bags?"

"My cash register receipts. The envelopes have all of my other stuff. Medical bills. Interest payments. Insurance."

"I know I'm going to hate myself for asking, but what's in the purse?"

"Contributions to charity. You know like when you're driving along, and somebody's on a street corner collecting for muscular dystrophy and you give 'em a dollar."

"You actually kept track of that? I'm impressed," he said, opening the purse. He pulled out a Popsicle stick with "$2/M.D." scribbled on it, followed by a button from the heart fund drive clipped to a scrap of paper that said 50 cents. There were also stubs for at least a dozen charity raffles and the ends from three boxes of chocolate mint Girl Scout cookies. He groaned.

"What's wrong?" Victoria demanded. "It's all very clear."

"Yes. I suppose it is," Tate admitted. "It's just that I'm used to..."

"You're used to nice, tidy books with columns of numbers that all add up."

The way she put it sounded insulting, as though there was something wrong with believing in order. "I can't help it if I've been trained to respect reliable accounting methods. This is...it's..." He couldn't even find a word to express his utter dismay at her lackadaisical approach to record keeping.

"Mr. McAndrews," Victoria said, her cheeks flushed and her blue eyes flashing. "I have better things to do with my time than write a bunch of figures down in some book. They all add up the same whether they're in a book or in that shopping bag."

Tate's head was starting to pound. He was beginning to feel the way he had earlier when he'd understood her logic in expecting that ridiculous tax refund. "I suppose," he agreed without very much conviction. He stood up and tried to balance the stack of shoeboxes in one arm, while grabbing the two shopping bags and the purse with the other. He motioned toward the envelopes. "Can you get those?"

"Where are you going with this?"

"I'm going to take it into the office and try to make some sense of it. That's what an audit is all about. I have to assure the IRS that you haven't tried to cheat them."

Victoria sighed. "I haven't, you know," she said softly, her voice filled with something that sounded like disappointment at his continued disbelief.

Tate nodded. Ironically, he did believe her. No one whose head was as high in the clouds as Victoria Marshall's would ever dream of cheating on her taxes. And even if the thought had crossed her mind, he doubted if she could figure out how to do it.

Victoria followed him down the stairs and out to his car, noting that it was what she would have expected him to drive: a very conservative, American made, four-door sedan. Anyone with his precise, orderly mind definitely would not be into flash and dazzle. She was a little worried, though, about the effect the afternoon seemed to have had on him. He did not look like the same determined, self-confident man who'd walked into her life a few hours earlier. He appeared defeated somehow, though his brown eyes did twinkle a little when he said goodbye.

"What happened to dinner?" she taunted. "I did win the bet, you know."

"As soon as I figure this out, I'll be in touch," he promised with a sizzling, sensual smile that sent her blood pressure soaring. "And we'll celebrate your victory over IRS with champagne, caviar and beef Wellington."

As he drove off, Victoria sighed. If he threw in candlelight and roses, she'd be a goner.

Three

The following morning, Victoria sat at the kitchen table for a long time, dreamily sipping a cup of tea and trying unsuccessfully to push disturbing and unexpectedly lusty thoughts of Tate McAndrews from her mind. The rumpled tan sports jacket he'd forgotten and left draped over the back of a chair was not helping matters. When she'd run her hand over the fine material, her fingers had picked up the lingering, tangy scent of his cologne. The clean, outdoorsy odor had brought back a sharp image of that brief, tantalizing moment when he'd caught her and held her in his arms.

Of all the men who might have wandered into her life and stirred up her untapped passions, Tate McAndrews was the worst possible choice. Tate was so...sensible, so practical. She had the distinct impression that he would never do anything impulsive. He would examine all the implications, evaluate the possible consequences and then, if it didn't seem too costly, he might indulge in a few minutes of simple fun.

She, on the other hand, was constantly getting sidetracked by interesting, unexpected things. Not once could she ever recall going from point A to point B without wandering off to explore along the way. She saw life in glorious, spectacular Technicolor. If what she'd seen yesterday was any indication, Tate seemed to view it in black and white, without the benefit of any grays.

Victoria sighed. It was definitely a mismatch. And yet.... She glanced over at the bright yellow wall phone, dared it to ring, then shook her head.

"You are losing it, Victoria," she muttered aloud. "It's barely 8:00 a.m. No man, however enchanted he might be, is likely to call at that hour, and Tate McAndrews did not seem the least bit enchanted." She paused thoughtfully, recalling those one or two looks that could have sizzled bacon to a crisp. She shook her head and dismissed them. "Uh-uh. The man thinks you are a certifiable nut. There is a very good chance he will not call at all...unless he remembers his jacket or decides to haul you in for income tax evasion. Forget about him."

Deep down she knew this was good advice. She also knew she wasn't likely to follow it. Unfortunately romantics never listened to their heads. Lancelot, who had finished his breakfast and retreated to the windowsill for his morning sunbath, meowed softly as though in complete agreement with her analysis of the absurdity of her behavior.

"Oh, shut up, cat! Don't you start on me," she grumbled irritably, slamming down her teacup and grabbing the morning paper. She turned the pages with a vengeance that caused more than one of them to tear. When the phone shrilled a moment later, she jumped nervously and stared at it, almost afraid to pick it up.

"Hello," she said at last, her voice soft, low and unintentionally sexy.

"Victoria? Is that you? You sound like you have a cold."

"Oh. Hi, Mom," she said, unconsciously trading sexiness for disappointed grumpiness.

"My goodness, that's certainly a cheerful greeting. What's wrong with you?"

"Nothing," she denied, trying to inject a little spirit into her voice before her mother rushed over with chicken soup and parental advice. "I'm fine. What's up?"

"I was just wondering if you'd like a little company at the shop today. I haven't seen you in a while."

"Three days."

"Well, it seems like longer."

Victoria chuckled. She knew how her mother loved to help out at the shop. She enjoyed meeting the people, and she absolutely loved haggling with them over a price. She said it made up for the frustration of having to pay outrageous prices without question in the local stores.

"Come on over, Mom. I should be there about ten."

"Why don't I stop by and pick you up? There's no point in driving two cars."

"I gather you're planning to spend the day?" Victoria teased.

Katherine Marshall refused to rise to the bait. "I thought I might as well. Your father had to go up to Columbus on business, and you did say you wanted to do some refinishing work in the back on that new washstand you bought last week."

"Why don't you say it, Mom?"

"Say what?"

"That you think you're better at the business side of running the shop than I am."

"Dear, surely even you must agree that you are a bit casual about making the best possible deal. I swear, sometimes I think you'd give something away just because someone admired it."

"I like my pieces to go to people who'll treasure them," she said defensively. "Not just to the highest bidder."

"Hasn't it ever occurred to you that the highest bidder must like something very much to pay so dearly for it?"

"I suppose. But it seems so..."

"Businesslike?"

"Okay, okay. You've made your point," Victoria said, wishing her mother didn't sound quite so much like Tate McAndrews. She had a feeling if the two of them ever joined forces, her life would become a boring, organized regimen of computerized bookkeeping. The very thought made her shudder. "If you promise to drop the lecture, you can come on over and pick me up."

"I'll be there in a few minutes," her mother replied tartly. "But I won't promise to keep my mouth shut."

She hung up before Victoria could respond.

As Victoria dressed in a pair of oversized, paint-splattered coveralls appropriate for the refinishing work she needed to do, she thought about her shop. Located just outside of town in the front of a large, converted barn, it had been open less than a year. She'd started the venture at her parents' enthusiastic urging. She'd accumulated so many interesting odds and ends at garage and farm sales that she'd run out of space to store them. In fact, her parents' garage had become so cluttered that for three months in the dead of a very snowy winter they'd been unable to get their car inside. At first they had dutifully admired the battered, scratched treasures she had dragged home. But after digging the car out of snowdrifts more than once, they had begun dropping subtle hints that these wonderful finds of hers would look much better "someplace where they could be displayed to advantage. Perhaps even sold."

The idea of selling something she'd discovered in a dusty old attic or in the back corner of some other shop had vaguely disturbed Victoria. She'd bought these things because she'd loved each and every one of them. Only after her mother had reminded her that she couldn't very well afford to hoard every antique in southern Ohio had she agreed to consider the idea.

The more she'd thought about it, the better she had liked it.

Once the plan had taken hold in her mind, she went about it with her usual high-spirited enthusiasm, spending a small inheritance from her grandmother to rent the perfect, old, unused barn on the Logan property and to renovate it. At first she'd only been open on weekends, continuing to teach history during the week. Soon she had quit her job at the high school and kept the shop open Tuesdays through Sundays. Her mother willingly filled in whenever she needed to go to an auction or wanted to take some time off.

"Victoria!" Her mother's shouted greeting broke into her reverie.

"I'll be down in a minute, Mom." She ran a brush hurriedly through her hair, then twisted it into a loose knot on top of her head. Golden-red curls promptly escaped in every direction. She tried taming a few of them, then gave it up as a lost cause. "So, I look like Little Orphan Annie. I'm going to refinish a washstand, not try out for Miss Ohio."

When she ran down the stairs and skidded to a halt in the kitchen a few minutes later, her mother was holding Tate's jacket out in front of her as though it were a live snake.

"This is not your father's," she said emphatically.

Victoria couldn't help grinning at her puzzled expression. "Nope," she said, opening the door of the refrigerator and sticking her head inside to scout around for some yogurt to take along for lunch.

"Victoria!"

She peeked around the side of the door. "Yes, Mother?"

"Whose jacket is this?"

Somehow Victoria did not want to explain about the IRS audit or about Tate. Her mother would want to hire an entire office of attorneys to defend her, and she wasn't quite up to fighting with her about it. "A friend's," she replied vaguely, sticking her head back in the refrigerator. She wasn't sure how long she could spend deciding between black cherry and lemon yogurt, but she was hoping it would be enough time to chill her mother's questions.

"What friend?"

She sighed. Obviously, her mother did not intend to drop the topic until her curiosity had been fully satisfied. Victoria gave up the idea of hiding and slammed the refrigerator door. Her nose had been getting cold anyway. "A man, Mother."

"I can tell it's a man, young lady. What are you trying to hide? Are you involved with someone? Is it serious? Why haven't your father and I met him?"

"Mother, I only met him myself yesterday."

Her mother's eyes widened. "You only met this man yesterday, and he's already leaving clothes lying around your house?"

"It is not what it seems."

Katherine Marshall looked at her skeptically. "Are you quite sure?"

"Now you sound disappointed, Mother. Are you that anxious to be rid of me?"

"I am not anxious to be rid of you. I would like to see you settle down with some nice, sensible young man who could take care of you."

The description certainly fit Tate, but Victoria was not about to get her mother's hopes up. Given the slightest provocation, her mother was capable of planning maneuvers that would terrify and subdue an entire company of marines, much less a lone IRS agent. "I do not need someone to take care of me. I have a home—"

"Such as it is."

Victoria shot her a reproachful glance. "I have a business—"

"Which you run like a front yard lemonade stand."

"And I have my friends—"

"Who are all nuttier than you are."

"Mother, I'm so glad you are on my side."

Katherine Marshall beamed at her, ignoring her sarcastic tone. "You should be dear. But I won't be around forever, and I'd like to know there's someone who'll look after you and keep you out of mischief when I'm gone."

"You're healthier than I am, so I don't think that's something we need to worry about today. Now could we drop this subject and get over to the shop? You may be missing a sale."

"Oh, dear. Of course, you're right." She put the jacket back on the chair. "But Victoria, I want you to promise me that you'll bring this young man of yours over to meet your father and me."

"Mother, I solemnly swear that if this man ever becomes *my young man*, you and Dad will be the first to hear. Just so you know, though, you will not have the power of a veto." Not that that was likely, she thought dryly.

When they pulled into the driveway at the shop a few minutes later, the young man in question was pacing around the barn much to her amazement and dismay. His very neat and very flattering navy pin-striped suit looked totally out of place in the rural setting. Victoria wondered curiously if he even owned a pair of blue jeans. Then she caught sight of the mud caked on his expensive leather shoes and winced. If Tate planned to keep up these visits, he obviously needed to get a new, more practical wardrobe before he destroyed the one he had.

"Is that the young man?" Katherine Marshall hissed, as her daughter opened the car door and got out. Victoria rolled her eyes heavenward. These were not the circumstances she'd had in mind for a second meeting with Tate McAndrews.

"Do you always show up for work an hour late?" he was demanding irritably, a scowl on his handsome face.

"I have an 'in' with the owner," she responded tartly, as she unlocked the door and stalked inside.

"That is no way to—"

"Run a business," Katherine Marshall chimed in. "I've been telling her that very thing myself. Hello. I'm Victoria's mother."

She held out her hand and waited expectantly. Tate took it, then looked in amazement from this trim, tidy woman with the firm handshake and no-nonsense style to Victoria in another one of her outrageous getups. He'd never have believed it. This woman seemed perfectly... normal. She would never keep her bills in shopping bags.

"Tate McAndrews," he told her. "I'm from—"

"Tate is a friend from Cincinnati," Victoria interrupted quickly, shooting him a warning glance. "I'm surprised to see you again so soon."

"I needed to talk to you about—"

"Dinner."

"Oh, is Victoria making you dinner tonight, Tate?" Katherine Marshall asked cheerfully. "How lovely. Why don't the two of you drop by the house for dessert?"

"Mother!"

"We'd love to, Mrs. Marshall."

"Are you out of your mind?" Victoria snapped at him, marching into the back room with Tate trailing after her.

"What's wrong with you? I was just trying to be polite."

"Don't you realize that if we go over there for dessert tonight, my mother will have the church reserved by next weekend? She already thinks we're involved," she told him, her brows lifting significantly. "That's in capital letters, by the way."

"Involved?" Tate repeated, his expression completely baffled. "You mean...?" His eyes widened as the implication finally registered. "Why on earth would she think that?"

"Your jacket."

"My jacket?" Tate was getting that spinning sensation in his head again.

"You left it in the kitchen. My mother, the protector of my virtue, found it there this morning. She's assumed the worst."

Tate burst out laughing. He couldn't help it. "You're kidding!"

"I do not kid about matters such as marriage and murder, particularly when they're my own."

"Can we expect to find your father on the front porch with a shotgun?"

Victoria gave him a withering glance. "Okay," she warned. "Make fun of me. But I'm telling you, before you know it, that woman in there is going to have you marching down the aisle."

"I'm a total stranger."

"She doesn't know that."

"She would not try to marry her daughter off to someone she doesn't even know."

"Tate, my mother may seem quiet and unassuming to you, but in her heart lurks the soul of a desperate matchmaker."

"Why should she be desperate? You're hardly over the hill."

"Thanks. But she seems to think I have all the characteristics of a woman who's going to spend her whole life in trouble up to her eyebrows without some man to protect her."

"That thought has crossed my mind, too."

"See what I mean?" she said triumphantly. "You're two of a kind. Once she finds that out, you and I will have no further say in this. You might as well go back to Cincinnati and start picking out silver patterns."

"Actually, I saw one out front I thought was rather nice," he taunted.

Victoria groaned and buried her head in her arms. "I don't believe this."

Tate was watching her closely, and something in the vulnerable curve of her neck got to him. Tentatively, he ran his fingers along the soft, tender skin. "I don't believe it, either," he said huskily.

She gazed up at him with luminous blue eyes and wondered why on earth she'd been putting up such a fuss. It wasn't as though Tate was some disgustingly ugly, boring toad. He was a handsome prince, if ever she'd seen one, but he was so blasted unsuitable. He would never pick daisies with her or wade barefoot in a stream or ride a merry-go-round, at least not without thinking twice about it.

He leaned down and brushed a soft kiss across her lips, igniting a flame that first flickered weakly, then burst into a glorious heat. "Oh," she sighed softly, as his lips captured hers again, this time more hungrily. Only their mouths touched, but it was a possessive branding.

Then, just when Victoria started seeing an entire kaleidoscope of colors, Tate stood up, his expression thoroughly confused and somewhat horrified. "I'm sorry."

"Why?" she asked curiously.

"I shouldn't have done that."

"Didn't you enjoy it?" For some reason, she couldn't resist teasing him. She knew exactly why he was so disturbed. His behavior had been both unpredictable and, from what she suspected about IRS regulations, unprofessional. Tate McAndrews did not strike her as the type to bend, much less break, the rules.

"Of course, I enjoyed it."

"Well, then?"

"It's just not . . ."

"Proper? I promise you I won't charge you with sexual harassment." She held up her hand solemnly, though her lips were twitching.

"That's not the point."

"Don't you ever do anything because it feels right at the moment?"

"Of course," he said stiffly, thinking of the majority of his relationships. They were all built on a flimsy base of such moments without a single solid thread to hold them together. That had never bothered him before. Why did it suddenly seem so shallow and unfulfilling?

"That's encouraging," Victoria was saying cheerfully.

"Is it? I'm not so sure," he said honestly.

"Tate, why did you come here today?"

"I needed to ask you a question about your tax return."

"Couldn't you have called?"

He looked at her oddly. "I suppose so."

"Why didn't you?"

He appeared genuinely puzzled. "I'm not sure."

Victoria patted his arm. "That's okay. Don't worry about it. Why don't you sit down, and I'll bring you a nice cup of tea, and we can discuss my taxes to your heart's content?"

Suddenly the idea of discussing taxes with Victoria bored him to tears. What he really wanted was to kiss her again and, quite probably, again.

"I think I'd better be going."

"But you just got here."

"No," he corrected. "You just got here. I've been here over an hour, and now I have to get back to work."

"But you haven't asked me any questions yet."

"I'll ask them over dinner."

Victoria's eyes widened. "You're still planning to come for dinner?"

"Of course." He grinned at her. "And for dessert with your parents."

"Maybe it would be better if I wrote a letter to the IRS and told them to forget about the $15,593."

"And twelve cents," he reminded her. "Uh-uh. It's too late."

She moaned. "I was afraid of that."

Tate leaned down and brushed a kiss across her forehead. "See you later."

Victoria nodded.

"And try not to get in any more trouble."

She nodded again as he walked through the door into the front of the shop. As she heard him laughing with her mother, Victoria sighed. "Why do I have the feeling I'm already in so much trouble it would take Indiana Jones and Superman to get me out?"

Four

Victoria had just stepped out of the bathtub when she heard the doorbell ring. She glanced at the clock as she padded across the bedroom to peer out the front window. It was six o'clock on the dot. Of course, Tate McAndrews would never be late. He'd probably arrived in the world precisely nine months to the second after his conception. Right now he was pacing impatiently outside, a frown wrinkling his very attractive brow as he stopped to test each board that creaked under his weight. She had a feeling she was in for another one of his lectures, this one a double-barreled poke at both her house and her tardiness.

Victoria knew that punctuality was considered a socially desirable trait, and she really meant to try harder to attain it, but events always conspired against

her. Tonight, for example, she'd gotten home right on
time, despite another afternoon shower that had
turned the driveway at the shop into a sea of mud that
had almost trapped her mother's car. She'd planned
to fix a plain, but hearty stew and some homemade
buttermilk biscuits for dinner, take a leisurely, fragrant bubble bath and find the perfect outfit for this
absurd date Tate had trapped her into.

But as she'd started to dice the onions and chop the
carrots, she'd glanced out the kitchen window and
seen this glorious rainbow that disappeared right over
the crest of the hill. She couldn't resist trying to find
the end of it. By the time she'd run barefoot through
the damp grass to the far side of the hill and back
again, her schedule was all out of kilter...as usual.

She threw open the bedroom window and leaned
out. "Come on in," she called down cheerfully. "The
door's open."

Horrified by such a casual announcement indicat-
ing an absolute lack of concern for her own safety,
Tate's gaze flew up and encountered those dancing
blue eyes and a considerable amount of bare white
flesh shimmering with droplets of water. His stern re-
tort on the dangers of leaving her front door unlocked died on his lips as his heart lurched crazily. This
woman's unabashed innocence was far more provocative than any planned seduction he'd ever encountered. How could she possible not know the effect
she'd have leaning out that window with a blue towel
precariously draped around her and that red halo of
hair spilling over her creamy shoulders? Yet he knew
with absolute certainty that she had no idea that she

was even capable of provoking a very masculine response in him. It was one of her more charming traits.

Some of her other habits were ... He tried to think of a kind description and couldn't. Infuriating was the first word that came to mind. Maybe also baffling or irresponsible, he thought, his anger returning. Like leaving her door unlocked as though the entire world were trustworthy. Didn't she read the newspapers?

"I'll be down in a minute," she promised, and Tate swallowed his irritation and resigned himself to a half hour—minimum—of waiting. He should have known her lateness this morning hadn't been an exception. A woman like Victoria would never be on time. He was probably lucky she was even home.

He walked in the front door and debated where he should wait. Poking his head in what he'd decided yesterday was the living room, he glanced again at the disreputable and uncomfortable looking sofa and promptly opted for the kitchen, where he'd expected to find all sorts of tantalizing smells coming from the oven and from pots simmering on the stove. A woman who prided herself on offering all sorts of delicacies to her customers would surely cook a spectacular dinner. His mouth had been watering all afternoon.

Instead of finding a gourmet feast, however, the only hints of dinner preparations were a diced onion and a bunch of partially chopped carrots scattered across a cutting board on the counter. The air was filled only with the sweet scent of lilacs and something else he couldn't quite identify. It smelled faintly fishy. He sniffed and his nose wrinkled in dismay. What on earth was it? Not dinner, he hoped.

He heard a soft, appealing meow and felt something nudging his ankles hopefully. A puff of gray fur wound itself between his legs. There was another meow, this one louder and definitely more demanding.

"Hey, old guy, are you starving, too?" he inquired, before suddenly realizing that the subtle odor had been that of cat food. "You can't be, you old fake. You've obviously been fed. Don't try to trick me into giving you a second dinner."

Lancelot, apparently sensing that he was wasting his friendliness, gave Tate a haughty look of disgust and walked away, his tail switching. Tate chuckled at the cat's indignant departure. Victoria and Lancelot were obviously two of a kind.

"If you don't mind, you could finish chopping the carrots." Victoria's musical voice drifted down to him. He had a feeling she could talk a man into chopping down trees. Carrots were no problem at all. "I won't be long."

Lured by the sound of that voice, Tate wandered out to the front of the stairs. "Anything else?"

"There are some potatoes around somewhere. You could try to find them and peel them."

"Do I get any clues?"

"About what?"

"Where they might be."

"They might be in the refrigerator," she suggested, as Tate started toward the kitchen again. "Wait. No. I think I put them in the pantry." He paused and waited. "On second thought, try under the sink."

He rolled his eyes heavenward and sighed. "Are the potatoes important?"

"Of course. I'm making a stew. It probably won't be very good, though. It should have been simmering for the last hour."

"What happened? Did you get held up at the shop?"

"No. I got home right on time, but there was this rainbow...." Her voice trailed off as Tate groaned and returned to the kitchen, reminding himself for the fiftieth time since yesterday that this woman was obviously not his type.

"So, why are you here, McAndrews?" he muttered under his breath. His pulse speeded up as an image of her scantily clad body flitted through his mind. He scowled. "That's a lousy answer."

He yanked open the refrigerator door and looked for the potatoes. He tried the pantry next, then checked the cabinet under the sink. He gave up, then accidentally found them when he opened the back door to let Lancelot out. They were sitting on the steps. He shrugged resignedly. "It's as good a place as any, I suppose."

By the time Victoria finally got downstairs, he had finished with the carrots and peeled the potatoes. The finished product didn't look quite right to him, but what did he know about peeling things? Apparently not much, judging from the quirk of amusement that tilted Victoria's soft, coral lips when she saw them. His earlier desire to sweep her straight into his arms returned with a nearly uncontrollable urgency, startling him into a subdued silence as he simply stared at her.

"You don't spend a lot of time in the kitchen, do you?" she said dryly, as she unceremoniously plopped his efforts into a huge pot, added some water, onions and already browned beef that she'd plucked from the refrigerator. Then she liberally sprinkled dibs and dabs of various spices over the top, her brow puckered in concentration.

"It shows?"

"It shows," she confirmed, glancing over at him. "Who fixes your meals for you?"

"I go out a lot."

"What about breakfast? Are you any better at that?"

"Not much."

"Then what...?" Her voice trailed off as he began to grin. "Never mind."

"I eat cereal," he informed her, as her cheeks turned decidedly pink. "At home."

"Oh," she said softly, an unfortunate tone of relief in her voice. He was still grinning...openly chuckling, in fact.

For the first time since he'd arrived, Victoria took a really good look at Tate. He was wearing the same shirt and suit pants he'd had on this morning. Even his tie was right in place, and his shoes had been polished to a high gloss without a trace left of this morning's muddy excursion around her barn. He had rolled up his sleeves to attack the potatoes and carrots, but that was the only concession to comfort he'd made.

His formality, combined with the odd way he was looking at her, made Victoria even more uncomfortable than she already had been about having this man back in her kitchen. There was a raw hunger in his eyes she couldn't quite identify, but it made her decidedly nervous. Maybe he was crazy about stew and couldn't wait for her to get dinner on the table. She gazed into his eyes again and blinked at the intensity. No, she thought, that look had nothing to do with food.

"Don't you ever wear anything besides a suit?" she finally asked, her voice far shakier than she would have liked.

"Sure, but not when I'm working."

She quirked a brow at him. "You're working now?"

"Of course. Until this audit is finished, any meeting we have is part of the investigation."

"Shouldn't I call an attorney or something, then?" she taunted.

That look in his eyes faded as he scowled at her. "I don't plan to arrest you, for heaven's sakes."

"You're going to charge me with tax evasion or fraud or something equally unpleasant."

"I told you yesterday, I believe you didn't do anything illegal. But once the case is opened, there are procedures we have to follow."

"You probably never speed either," she said wearily.

"Not often," he admitted, suddenly wishing he had at least a parking ticket he could tell her about.

"Haven't you ever wanted to break just one little rule?"

"There are reasons for rules."

"Do you always agree with those reasons?"

"Of course not."

"Then what do you do?"

"Try to get the rules changed."

Victoria tried to imagine Tate in the middle of a protest rally. Not even her vivid imagination could come up with an impression of that scene. He probably made an appointment, sat down and discussed things rationally, shook hands politely and waited for change to take place. The people he approached probably listened too. She had a feeling he could be a very persuasive man when he wanted to be.

He was sitting at the kitchen table now, his hands braced behind his head, leaning back in the chair and watching her again, laughter dancing in his dark brown eyes. She had a feeling he found her amusing and that irritated the daylights out of her. Despite her misgivings about all of this, she'd wanted to be beautiful and sexy and alluring tonight. She'd searched her closet and found a lovely old dress with tiny sprigs of bright yellow flowers on a beige background. It had a scooped neck, edged with antique lace, that drew attention to her full breasts and a wide satin sash that emphasized her tiny waist. For once, her hair had cooperated and fallen into shining waves. And now this infuriating man was laughing at her. She felt like smacking him in the mouth. Instead, she sliced through a tomato with a whack that jarred the counter.

Tate winced. "Remind me never to make you angry."

Victoria grinned. "You just did."

"How?" he asked.

"You were laughing at me."

"I was?"

"Weren't you?"

"I was smiling."

"At me."

Tate's head started spinning again. "Actually I was thinking about how unusual you are. I've never met a woman like you before." At the moment, he wasn't sure if that was good or bad.

"And that made you laugh."

"Smile."

"Whatever," she said airily. She hesitated for a minute, then confessed, "I was going for sexy."

"Ahh," he said softly as an even broader grin split his face. "Now I see."

The knife sliced through another tomato with a resounding thwack.

"You are sexy, you know," he said almost casually. Victoria promptly nicked her finger with the knife.

"Damn!"

"What happened?" He was out of his chair and at her side in an instant.

"Nothing. Nothing at all."

"Let me see."

"It's just a little cut. I do this all the time," Victoria lied. There was no way she was going to let him think that he'd rattled her by telling her he thought she was sexy. It wasn't a complete lie, anyway. She did nick her fingers constantly. She had this dangerous habit of letting her mind wander while she was fixing meals.

"Let me see it," he repeated insistently, a look of steely determination in his eyes.

Reluctantly, she held out her hand. The tiny cut had already stopped bleeding.

"Do you have some antiseptic? And you'll need a bandage."

"Don't be ridiculous. It's practically healed already."

"Have you had a tetanus shot?"

Obviously he planned to ignore her protests and turn this into a case for a trauma unit, she thought resignedly. Maybe he was a frustrated paramedic.

"I think so."

"When?"

"I don't know."

"Then we ought to take you to the hospital," he said decisively, confirming her worst expectations.

"Tate McAndrews!" Victoria suddenly bellowed. "Sit down!"

Tate's eyes widened, but he sat back down. Victoria faced him with her hands on her hips. "Now will you please relax. Loosen your tie. Have a drink. Go upstairs and try to organize my bills. Anything, but please don't hover over me. I already have two perfectly good parents to do that."

"Did I touch a sore spot?" he asked innocently.

Victoria gave him a wobbly smile. "Well, they are a bit overly protective. You'll see."

"I brought them a bottle of Scotch, by the way."

"They don't drink."

Dismay suddenly filled Tate's eyes. That look of uncertainty, which gave a surprising impression of vulnerability, touched her. She wanted to pat his hand.

"I knew I should have brought candy," he muttered.

"You didn't need to bring anything."

"Of course I did. I read Miss Manners."

"If you're so worried about making a good impression on my parents, do me a favor."

"Anything."

"When we get over there tonight, don't say anything about working for the IRS or about this audit."

Tate looked at her oddly. "I gathered this morning that you wanted to keep this some deep, dark secret. Why? They're your parents."

"Exactly. They'll only worry, and I can handle it on my own."

"What if you can't?"

Victoria looked at him, a frown creasing her forehead. "You said you believed me."

"I do, but I'm not the only one involved."

"But you'll do the report. Won't they take your word for it?"

Tate hesitated. "Usually they do."

"Well, then. You see," she said, flashing him a wide smile that lit her blue eyes with glittering highlights. "I have nothing to worry about."

Tate couldn't bring himself to tell her that if Pete Harrison got even the tiniest inkling of the attraction he felt toward her, he'd put four other agents on the case to check out his work. Pete did not believe his agents should have human emotions. Anyone who did was suspect. In fact, if they could program computers to do the legwork, instead of just the analysis, Pete would happily fire his entire staff.

Tate glanced at Victoria and felt his stomach muscles tighten at the perfect picture she presented. All of her worries over the audit were apparently forgotten thanks to her faith in his ability to protect her. She hummed cheerfully while stirring the stew. Norman Rockwell would have loved having her as a model. Her cheeks were flushed from the fragrant steam now rising from the pot. Golden-red curls framed her face. As she lifted the spoon to her mouth and tasted the stew, her lips pursed in an enchanting frown. Her hand hovered over the spice rack, then plucked out two bottles and sprinkled a dash of the contents into the pot. She tried the stew again and shook her head.

"It's still missing something. You taste it."

She dipped out a steaming spoonful and brought it to Tate, who obediently opened his mouth. Her eyes were on his lips as they closed over the spoon, and she ran her tongue over her own in an unconsciously sensual gesture that did all sorts of crazy things to Tate's pulse rate. He had a sudden urge to take the spoon out of her hand, pull her into his lap and taste the softness of her mouth for himself. Surely, it was more delectable than any stew. His eyes, filled with a raw yearning he couldn't disguise, lifted to meet hers, and he saw that she shared his hunger. He also saw that it seemed to startle her. She blinked and turned back to the stove, her hand shaking so badly that the spoon clattered against the side of the pot.

"I think the stew tastes fine," he said softly.

"Are you sure?"

"Absolutely."

She shrugged. "Okay. Then I think we're about ready. We were supposed to have biscuits, but I ran out of time."

She brought a loaf of homemade bread to the table instead and added a crock of fresh butter, then dished up huge steaming bowls of the stew. Over dinner, as the conversation veered off on one crazy tangent after another, Tate realized they had at least a few things in common, though hardly the sort of list that would qualify them for a computerized matchup. More important than their skimpy selection of mutual favorite things were the sparks that flew during lively discussions of their disagreements. Victoria had a razor sharp intelligence under that zaniness. She listened carefully to Tate's point of view and actually tried to understand it. Of course, she then dismissed it with some totally illogical argument that he could barely follow. When she started to make sense it scared the living daylights out of him.

Still, it was a beginning. But of what? A friendship? A brief romance? Surely it could be no more than that. They'd drive each other crazy, just as his parents had. His mother's disorganization, her off-the-wall logic and her absolute refusal to think beyond the moment had given his father fits. And, much as he loved his mother, Tate had agreed with his father. Life was supposed to have an order, a certain logic to it. You had to be able to count on things.

He glanced up at Victoria, who was stacking dishes haphazardly on the counter. She was definitely not a woman who knew the first thing about order. He sighed as a plate slipped off the counter and crashed to the floor.

"Let me help," he said, bending down to pick up the pieces.

"I've got it."

Their hands closed over the same piece and their eyes met. The already charged atmosphere sizzled with electricity. Almost against his will, Tate leaned slowly forward and kissed her. He meant it only to be a light, teasing kiss, the sampling of her honeyed sweetness that he'd wanted all evening. Instead, it virtually crackled with passion. The piece of china fell back to the floor, as Victoria's hands slid slowly along his arms, finally coming to rest lightly on his shoulders. His own hands circled her tiny waist and lifted her to her feet, pulling her body tightly against his. The curves seemed to fit perfectly into his hard contours, as though a sculptor had carved them as a matching pair out of a single piece of marble.

As her body trembled in Tate's muscular arms, Victoria remembered every passionate movie kiss she'd ever envied. She sighed, unconsciously opening her mouth to Tate's exploring tongue, relishing the sensation. The kiss was sweet yet hungry, gentle yet demanding. A riptide of warm, exciting feelings flooded through her, bringing her body alive in a most disconcerting way. She wanted more, wanted Tate's lips to move beyond her mouth, wanted his hands to touch the breasts that were straining against the thin cotton of her dress. She also wanted him to stop, to give her time to catch her breath. These feelings were too new,

too unexpected and far too powerful for her to deal
with quite yet.

"Tate," she murmured, as his lips blazed a path
down her neck. The fiery touch was even more intense, more nerve-shattering than she'd anticipated.
She moaned softly. "Tate, please. It's nearly eight."

"So?"

"We promised my parents we'd be there by eight."

"They think we're involved, remember. They'll understand."

His lips were at the crest of her breasts, hovering
over the creamy flesh. Victoria's body tensed in excited preparation for his touch, but she said firmly,
"No, they won't."

Tate kept one arm securely around her, locking her
body against his, as he glanced at his watch. "We're
not due there for another fifteen minutes."

"It's a twenty-minute drive."

"We could speed."

"You said you never broke the law."

"I don't, but I think this is worth an exception."

"I will not be responsible for your fall from grace,
Tate McAndrews," she said saucily, slipping determinedly from his embrace. "Besides, we need to talk
some more about this little visit we're about to pay to
my parents. I don't think you have any idea what
you're letting yourself in for."

"That's not exactly true," Tate denied with a weary
sigh of resignation. "When I came down here yesterday, I didn't. Now I know I'm in trouble. Your parents are just the tip of the iceberg."

Five

On the drive to her parents' house, Victoria tried to think of some way to make Tate understand that he was about to undergo a third degree that would make one of his IRS investigations seem like child's play. Every time she opened her mouth to explain, he told her to quit worrying. She finally shut up, but she didn't stop fretting.

She wasn't sure what concerned her the most: her mother's delighted, if mistaken, impression that she and Tate were involved or the possibility that her parents would discover that he was auditing her taxes. Either one posed a minefield of hazards that the man next to her couldn't possibly have considered when he innocently accepted her mother's invitation. She still didn't understand why he'd agreed to do that, much less why he'd wrangled that dinner invitation from her, but right now she didn't have time to puzzle that part out. She was far more concerned with this sinking feeling of dread that she was about to end the evening with either an entirely inappropriate fiancé or a companion who'd been hog-tied and sternly lectured until he agreed to drop his inquiry into her financial affairs.

"Tate, maybe we should forget about this," she suggested hopefully. "I'll explain to my parents that your malaria flared up again, and you were in no condition to drop in."

The look he gave her was withering. "I don't have malaria."

"They don't know that."

He glanced over at her, his expression puzzled. "It's just a friendly visit. Why are you making such a big deal about it?"

"Because my parents are going to make a big deal about it and you don't seem to be prepared."

"I've been dating since junior high school and been asked every conceivable parental question. They will not rattle me."

"First of all," she reminded him, "this is not a date."

"It isn't?"

"You said yourself it was part of the investigation," she said irritably, then added pointedly, "an investigation I don't want them to know about."

Tate frowned. "Well, it is part of the investigation...in a way."

"What does that mean?"

"It's not exactly official."

"Meaning you don't usually drop in for dinner when you're auditing someone's taxes."

"Right."

"Then it's a date after all?" she asked weakly, her head swimming. Dear Lord, this was getting complicated. Maybe *she* could develop malaria and go home.

Tate's frustrated expression reminded her of the way she felt. "That's what I said in the first place," he told her, sounding puzzled. "Isn't it?"

"I suppose," Victoria muttered, then sighed. "Okay, then. How many times have you been asked what your intentions are on a first date?" she challenged, then shrugged in defeat. "Oh, forget it. If you're crazy enough to want to go through with this, far be it from me to try to stop you. Turn here."

Tate pulled into the driveway of a lovely old farmhouse surrounded by towering oaks that were beginning to bud. Pale green sparkled in the early moonlight against the dark backdrop of massive trucks and mighty branches. Unlike Victoria's ramshackle house, this one looked as though it had been in top condition for a hundred years, its appearance so solid and dependable that Tate was sure it could withstand another hundred.

As he turned off the car's engine, the front door flew open, and Katherine Marshall stood framed in the doorway, her simple cotton print dress topped by a ruffled apron, her cheeks flushed prettily and her hair—a shade darker than Victoria's—coiled into a neat bun. As Tate and Victoria approached, she positively beamed at them. Tate thought she looked exactly the way a mother should look—comfortable, warm and assured. She looked like a mother who would bake cookies. His own mother had burned the one batch she'd ever tried and hired a cook the same afternoon. She'd told Tate she'd rather take him hang gliding and leave the baking to someone else. Having a mother who wanted to be his pal had given him a rather distorted view of things. He'd always yearned to come home from school to someone a bit more traditional.

"Tate, how wonderful that you could come. Victoria's father and I are so looking forward to getting to know you."

Tate saw no hidden meaning in the friendly words, but Victoria mumbled, "I warned you," under her breath. As her mother linked arms with him and drew him into the living room, he shot Victoria a reproachful glance before gazing down at her mother with a smile.

That's all I need, Victoria thought in disgust. A couple of hundred-watt smiles like that and my mother will start buying frames for pictures of the grandchildren. As the evening wore on, her mouth settled into a grim line. Tate was actually enjoying himself and her parents were clearly infatuated. They couldn't seem to believe that she had finally brought home someone who was down-to-earth and seemingly financially stable, someone her father could talk to and her mother could . . . well, mother.

When Katherine brought out warm apple cobbler topped with mounds of melting vanilla ice cream, Victoria knew for certain that wedding bells were already pealing in her head. Homemade cobbler was her mother's specialty, prepared only when she wanted to use her biggest guns to make a sure kill. The last time she'd baked one the town scrooge had forked over ten thousand dollars to beautify a park. He was still grumbling about Katherine Marshall's sly, under-handed tactics.

Tate caught the dismayed expression on Victoria's face and briefly wondered about it. Then he dismissed it as her father deftly steered the conversation over a fascinating range of topics—from the intrigues of small-town politics to rampant, unrestricted development and poor zoning, from bank failures to the national debt. All were things Tate understood and felt comfortable with. He'd grown up discussing these subjects with his own father. It was both nostalgic and satisfying to find someone older with whom he could share his thoughts again. He'd missed that since his father's death.

As for Mrs. Marshall, she reinforced his earlier impression of her straightforward, brutally honest approach to life. She was clearly a perfectly contented homemaker, a self-assured woman who would never whimper about life's harsh realities or pretend they didn't exist. She'd roll up her sleeves and pitch in to make things better, always with that sparkling sense of humor that made her bright blue eyes, that were so like her daughter's, crinkle with laughter.

Despite Victoria's dire warnings, he found the Marshalls to be exactly the kind of people he most enjoyed. It was Victoria herself who baffled him. How such an unconventional, impractical woman could have turned up on that very sensible family tree was beyond him. Yet though her parents teased her unmercifully about her more unique friends and crazy lifestyle, it was obvious that they doted on and worried about her. It gave him a warm feeling to see this much love, given so freely and unconditionally.

There was one awkward moment, which began when Katherine Marshall asked how he and Victoria had met.

"Well," he began and shot Victoria a look that cried out for help. He was not used to prevaricating and had no idea what he could say that wouldn't violate his promise to avoid mentioning the audit. She let him sit and squirm uncomfortably under her mother's interested gaze for several horrible seconds.

"It was an accident, Mother," she said when his nerves had stretched so taut he thought he'd have to blurt out the entire truth or explode.

Mrs. Marshall's eyes filled with concern. "An accident? You didn't wreck your car, did you? I've told you you should get rid of that old rattletrap. It's a menace."

"My car is not a menace and, anyway, it wasn't that kind of an accident. I'd just chased Lancelot up into a tree and got stuck. Tate came along and rescued me."

"Oh, my. How romantic," Mrs. Marshall said with a satisfied sigh, her eyes lighting with pleasure. "And how very fortunate that you happened by, Tate."

"Yes, that was a bit of luck, wasn't it?" Victoria said dryly. Tate refused to look her in the eye. He was terrified he would laugh and blow their tenuous credibility to smithereens.

Before he did, John Marshall tamped down the tobacco in his pipe with slow deliberation and said quietly, "Tell me, Tate, exactly what do you do for a living?"

"Ummm...I..."

"Tate's in finance," Victoria offered.

"Make a good living, do you?"

"Dad!"

Tate grinned. "Good enough."

"And you live in Cincinnati?"

"Yes."

"Like it there?"

"I've lived there all my life. It's a great city."

"You intend to stay there, then?"

"Well, yes, I suppose so."

"What about a family?" Katherine Marshall inquired, plopping another scoop of vanilla ice cream into his bowl and urging him to have a bit more cobbler.

Tate gulped. "I hadn't really thought about it," he said finally, as Victoria shot him an I-told-you-so look.

"A man can't wait too long to settle down," John Marshall said with all the subtlety of a rampaging rhino. He was obviously oblivious to Victoria's glare. Tate nodded politely, beginning to see exactly what he was up against. Oddly enough, the prospect of being bullied into a marriage with Victoria didn't terrify him nearly as much as it should have. Actually, the fact that it *didn't* was what scared him to death.

Despite the less than subtle nudging from the Marshalls, Tate found that he was having one of the best times of his life. From the incredible, mouth-watering apple cobbler to the gentle family teasing and intelligent conversation, he felt perfectly at home. Victoria, however, seemed to vacillate between amusement and nervousness. By the end of the evening, nervousness was winning out. The more Tate relaxed, the jumpier Victoria became. Soon he was certain that she'd been hoping they would all mix like oil and water. Then they'd never have to get together again.

When they were finally on the way home, after he'd promised to come back often, he questioned her about her odd attitude.

"You were hoping we'd hate each other, weren't you?"

"Why on earth would I want you to hate my parents?"

"You tell me."

She shook her head. "You're wrong. I expected you to like them. You're on the exact same wavelength," she said in a tone that made it sound as though they all were suffering from a similar incurable disease.

"Is that bad?"

She shrugged. "It is if you had other plans for the rest of your life."

"The marriage bit again," he said with a sigh. "It's crazy to worry about that. They can't push us into anything we don't want."

"Are you kidding? You are exactly what they've been looking for in a son-in-law. They're not about to let you get away. Didn't you notice the look of relief in my mother's eyes?'' She glowered at him, then added with an air of resignation. "No, of course you didn't. You were too busy trying to figure out why I'm not more like them.''

"The thought did cross my mind.''

She looked so sad when he said that that he wanted to take it back.

"I don't know why I'm not," she said wearily, as if it were something she'd though about often. "I try to be more organized. I really do, but it seems to escape me. There are always so many more interesting things going on. Maybe I'm a throwback to my grandmother. Everyone thought she was a little cracked too, just because she didn't believe in sitting back and letting life slip by. She had the time of her life. She went out and grabbed what she wanted, without giving a hoot if it was considered proper. The rest of the family was absolutely scandalized by her antics, but when she died at eighty-one, she had no regrets.

"I'm not going to have any either," she added defiantly, her eyes flashing a challenge at him.

"I wouldn't want you to,'' Tate countered, meeting her gaze head-on without flinching. He wondered briefly why it was so important for her to believe that.

Victoria seemed to consider the sincerity of his claim, then nodded. "No, maybe not. But you do think I should do things by the rules. I can tell from that funny little look you get in your eyes every time I do or say something you don't approve of. I know what you think of my bookkeeping and my house. You think I should computerize my records and live in some tidy little apartment with a fully equipped kitchen, wall-to-wall carpeting and a dead bolt lock on the door." She shivered.

Tate grinned at her apparent idea of a fate worse than death. "Would that be so awful?"

"Don't you see?" she said plaintively. "It wouldn't be me. Filling in all those little numbers bores me, and I like light and space and character in a house. I even like the fact that mine's a mess right now, because when I'm finished fixing it up, I'll know how much I've accomplished."

Tate didn't know what to say to that. Victoria waited for a response, then sighed and regarded him as though he were hopeless. "You loved their house, didn't you?"

"I'm not sure what that has to do with anything, but yes," he admitted.

Not only had the exterior been in perfect condition, the inside had been spotless, freshly painted in soft colors and decorated with a sense of symmetry. There hadn't been a magazine out of place. He wouldn't have changed a thing, including the intriguing collection of photos of Victoria from infancy through adolescence. She'd been a golden-haired cherub at birth and her evolution into a wickedly impish redhead had charmed him. The house had fairly shouted of family and tradition and dependability.

He sighed aloud at the memory and a soft smile curved his mouth. "I thought it was lovely."

"See. I knew it," Victoria huffed and then retreated into silence. She didn't say another word on the ride home, until they pulled to a stop in front of her house. Even then, she only mumbled an agreement to be in his office the following afternoon at two to wrap up the audit. She was out of the car before he could even begin to figure out what was wrong with her, much less try to take her in his arms and recapture the wildfire and magic of those first tentative kisses they'd shared earlier in the evening.

All night long Tate thought about the evening with the Marshalls, going over and over everything that had happened in his usual methodical way, trying to figure out why Victoria's impish humor had vanished. The evening had started out so well, and he hadn't been mistaken about those kisses in her kitchen. She was more than attracted to him. She had wanted him as much as he wanted her. Yet when they'd returned to her house, alone again at last, she couldn't get away from him fast enough.

He spent all morning at his desk shuffling papers and thinking about Victoria. His frustration and confusion, along with the sharp sexual tension in his abdomen that threatened to embarrass him, mounted all afternoon. He glanced up at the clock. It was 2:30 and Victoria was late again.

"Damn it," he grumbled moodily. "Why the devil can't she at least learn to be on time? Doesn't she own a watch?"

"Problems?" Pete Harrison inquired from the doorway in his gruff, raspy voice. That voice, combined with his perpetual scowl, gave the impression that he was always angry. Tate was one of the few people on his staff who suspected he wasn't.

"I thought that crazy dame who wanted the refund was due in here this afternoon," he said, staring at Tate pointedly. "Where is she?"

"She's late."

Pete seemed about to growl, then said mildly, "Hey, McAndrews, don't worry about it. What'd you expect from a kook?"

Tate had expected this particular kook to at least make an attempt to be on schedule just this once, since it was her taxes they were trying to straighten out. For Pete's benefit, he simply shrugged his agreement. There was no point in letting his boss know that he'd like to wring the woman's pretty little neck. Pete would think the uncharacteristic display of emotion highly suspicious. He'd moved Tate quickly through the ranks precisely because of his cool, calm, objective demeanor. Murdering the subject of an audit simply because she was late for an appointment did not qualify as objective—much less rational—behavior.

Despite his efforts to control it, some of his irritation apparently showed on his face anyway because Pete was regarding him suspiciously. "You okay, McAndrews? Is there a problem with this case I ought to know about?"

"What kind of problem could there be? You said it. The woman's a kook," he said, immediately feeling disloyal. If she was that much of a kook, then why was he so damned attracted to her? Why had he been sitting at his desk all morning watching the clock and counting the hours until her arrival, instead of working on another file? Much as he hated to admit it, he could hardly wait to see how she'd look today. He wondered if he'd find her as alluring as ever. Even worse, he could hardly wait to see what crazy, quirky tangent her mind would take. None of this he could admit to Pete.

Aloud, he said only, "I'll have the whole thing wrapped up in a day or two."

Pete nodded. "Good. I need you on something else next week, so don't waste any time." Pete muttered something else about wasting taxpayer dollars investigating dingy females as he wandered away, leaving Tate to glare angrily at the sweeping second hand of the clock as though it were responsible for Victoria's tardiness.

He had started pacing around his office like a caged lion when the door swung open, and Victoria breezed in wearing a dress that must have been in vogue at the turn of the century. Tate was getting used to these out-of-date costumes of hers. He realized it somehow suited her with its puffed sleeves, fitted waist and mid-calf skirt. Still, he glanced cautiously down to check for high-button shoes, but her feet, thankfully, were clad in perfectly ordinary black patent pumps. From those tiny feet and well-turned ankles, his gaze rose to her face, hoping for at least some sign of remorse. Instead, to his absolute fury, her eyes were sparkling with childlike excitement. His breath caught in his throat. Her sheer delight was almost contagious.

"Guess what?" she asked breathlessly, oblivious to his foul-tempered mood. She'd had the most wonderful morning. It had made her forget all about the uncomfortable evening she'd spent under the hopeful eyes of her parents. Today's sky had been a shimmering, cloudless blue. The recently tilled and planted fields were turning green and had the most marvelous, earthy smell. It had been absolute heaven to drive along and look at the change that spring had brought to the landscape. It had been all she could do to resist the urge to stop and pick wildflowers, but an image of Tate's disapproving scowl had kept her speeding along the country roads.

"Where have you been?" Tate practically shouted at her, making her wince, even though she'd been half expecting such a tirade.

She decided it would be better to ignore the question and his tone. He'd obviously had a bad morning, but, once he'd heard about hers, that grumpy mood would vanish.

"Wait until I tell you about this terrific new antique shop I found," she announced enthusiastically. "The owner used to be a teacher, just like me, and he spent his summers driving around the country hunting for antiques. Now that he's retired, he decided to open a shop in his home. And he had the most marvelous old dresser. It's a mess right now. It must have fifteen layers of paint on it, but the construction is solid—I think it's cherry—and it has the most beautiful beveled mirror. I'm having it picked up tomorrow. I can hardly wait to get to work on it. Oh, Tate, wait until you see it."

She gazed up at him expectantly, her smile wavering ever so slightly as she noticed that his scowl had not vanished as she'd hoped. "Is something wrong? I thought you'd be excited."

"You know I don't give a damn about antique dressers and beveled mirrors," he snapped. "When you make an appointment for two o'clock, you're supposed to arrive at two o'clock. Not two-forty-five."

"Ohhh. So that's it. Well, I'm here now, aren't I?" she said brightly, flashing him another brilliant smile and sitting down. The man definitely needed to get his priorities in order. In fact that was what had troubled her all last night. He was so single-minded. He didn't have an impulsive bone in his very attractive body.

To make matters worse, he fit in so neatly with her family and, much as she loved them, they weren't wildly impulsive either. More than anything they wanted to see her settled down with someone like Tate. If her parents had their way, they'd offer him a dowry just to reassure themselves that he'd take her on. She'd seen that thank-goodness-we've finally-found-someone look in their eyes even if Tate had been oblivious to it. He'd been so busy talking about strip zoning or something equally boring that he hadn't even noticed her mother practically measuring him for a tuxedo.

"Victoria," Tate began sternly, then sighed with frustration when he realized there was nothing he could say that would change her. "Oh, never mind. Let's get this over with."

But instead of proceeding in the brisk, businesslike manner he had in mind, Tate found that attempting to conduct a serious interview with Victoria was like trying to keep a toy train on a crooked track. She kept veering off in crazy, unexpected directions that at first infuriated, then delighted him. He listened raptly to one of her wild stories about leading her entire class of students in an all-night sit-in in the school cafeteria to give them a firsthand experience in Thoreau's concept of civil disobedience.

"What were you protesting?"

"The fact that they'd stopped serving hamburgers and fries."

"You staged a sit-in over hamburgers and French fries?"

"When you were a teenager, could you live without your daily ration of a burger, fries and a milk shake?"

"I can still live without them."

"I should have known," she said with a shake of her head. She studied him closely for several seconds, then smiled slowly. "Do you realize you haven't asked me a single dull question for the last half hour?"

"I haven't, have I?" he asked, his startled expression making her chuckle.

"It's wonderful," she told him approvingly.

"You won't think it's so wonderful when you have to go to court because I did a lousy job of finishing this audit and getting you off the hook."

"And the only way to do that is to ask boring questions?"

Tate nodded. "It would also help if I could get some straight answers."

"My answers are straight. I would never lie to you," she huffed.

"I'm not talking about lying. I'm talking about wandering all over the place with your answers until I'm so confused I find myself agreeing with you."

"Didn't it ever occur to you I might be right?"

"Not really."

"Thank you very much," she said, trying to keep the hurt out of her voice. She'd thought for a moment that Tate had actually approved of her. Instead, he'd only been laughing at her again. Well, that was just fine. She'd amuse him for another hour or so, straighten out this ridiculous mess, and then she'd drive home. That would be the end of it.

Except it wouldn't be. Something about this man appealed to her. Maybe it was nothing more than the crusader in her wanting to cure him of his stodginess and to discover if he had the stuff to be a true romantic hero. She sighed, wishing that was all there was to it. The real truth was that her suddenly traitorous body apparently didn't give a damn if he had the mind of a computer, as long as it could be held in those muscular arms and feel those sparks going off inside. She'd answer his ridiculous questions from now until doomsday just to reexperience the incredible feelings he aroused in her with one sizzling glance from those intense brown eyes. Right now those eyes were filled with laughter.

"You ready to try again?" he asked.

Victoria nodded reluctantly. "Fire away."

"I know I'm going to hate myself for asking this one, but explain to me how this contribution to somebody named Jeannie qualifies as charity."

Victoria couldn't help grinning at Tate's expression. He seemed to be holding his breath, obviously hoping for something he would consider a rational explanation. Well, this time she had one.

"Oh, that," she said airily. "Well, Jeannie is this friend of mine, who's trying to make it as an artist. You'll have to meet her sometime. She does ceramics. They're really quite special. She uses the loveliest blues and greens and grays." She paused thoughtfully, her lips pursed. "I can't quite figure out how she manages to get those shades, though I've watched and watched."

"Victoria," Tate said warningly.

She scowled, but went on. "Anyway, she wanted to help out Children's Hospital up in Columbus, only she didn't have any money. So I bought one of her pitchers, and she gave the money to the hospital," she concluded, gazing at him with eyes that seemed to expect him to understand how the leap from that transaction to her tax return made perfect sense. He supposed in her convoluted mind it did.

"Since the money went to the hospital, even though you gave it to Jeannie, you figured it was tax deductible," he said, trying not to scream.

"Exactly."

He shook his head. "Sorry."

"But the hospital qualifies as a charity," she protested vehemently.

"Jeannie doesn't."

"You don't know Jeannie," she mumbled.

"What does that mean?"

Her flashing gaze met his. "She's barely making ends meet, and she wanted to do something nice. I was only helping her out."

"And it was a wonderful gesture, but you can't deduct it," he said firmly.

"Oh, okay," she said, her voice edged with disgust. "Lordy, you people are picky."

"We're just following the rules."

Victoria sniffed and looked at him as though she'd like to tell him exactly what he could do with those rules. Tate promptly felt like an absolute rat and wished he'd gone into another profession. By the time the interview ended, he was worn out, and he knew his report to Pete Harrison was going to read like something from an anthology of science fiction.

Pete is never going to understand this, he thought, absolutely dazed and more intrigued than ever by this latest encounter with Victoria's logic. Something was happening to him and, for the life of him, he couldn't understand it. A sheer physical attraction he could deal with, but it was more than that. He was actually beginning to look forward to Victoria's slightly twisted train of thought. She was like the first crisp breeze of fall after a long, hot summer, a refreshing change that he'd never realized how much he'd longed for. Other women suddenly seemed so...ordinary. He grinned as he realized that he'd never before thought of that as an insult. He gazed at Victoria and something inside him seemed to snap. It was as though a belt that had been restricting the flow of blood had been suddenly loosened. He felt freer, happier than he'd felt in ages.

"Are we finished?" she asked him at last, blushing under his intense inspection.

"For now."

"And I can go?"

He stared at her, his expression clearly reflecting his disappointment. "Do you have to? I promised you a dinner."

Victoria's eyes widened. "You still want to take me?"

"Of course. I've been counting on it," he admitted, realizing it was true. He'd been thinking of nothing else all day long, and that was a first. Any woman who could get him to forget about his work, forget about business protocol for that matter, was a woman he needed to know better.

Or, he thought more rationally, one from whom he ought to be running like crazy.

He looked at Victoria, sitting across from him in her bright blue dress edged with black, her thick, red hair swept up in a Gibson girl style that emphasized her delicate features, and his breath came more rapidly...as though he'd already run a very long, very important race. And lost.

Six

Seated across from Tate in a lovely old restaurant where the lighting was seductively dim, the service impeccable and the food outrageously expensive, Victoria found herself relaxing and forgetting all about how totally inappropriate Tate was for her. The ambiance encouraged thoughts of romance. In fact, she had a feeling the tuxedo-clad waiters would escort anyone who seemed to be interested in anything else from the premises. Responding to the atmosphere, Tate's questions had lost the harsh edge of an inquisition and turned to more personal topics. It was as though he finally wanted to get to know her, not her tax status. He was going out of his way to be charming, displaying a surprising sense of humor and a willingness to poke fun at himself that she'd never suspected existed under the straitlaced exterior.

For the first time she had an idea of what it might be like to really date him, to feel his eyes sweep over her in a lingering visual caress, to hear his low voice whisper to her in a romantic undertone, to have him want her... and admit it. The idea intrigued her and a trembling responsiveness swept through her as she surveyed him in this new light.

Actually, she reminded herself, it wasn't so new. It was the way she had first viewed him from that tree and during those brief, tantalizing moments in his arms... right before they'd settled into their preassigned roles as righteous government worker and presumed tax evader. He had felt absolutely wonderful then, his body firm and solid and reassuring, his masculine muscles unyielding against her feminine softness. Just last night, his kisses had been the shattering, knee-weakening stuff of a torrid big screen love scene. A quiver of excitement flared at the memory, and suddenly she wanted more than anything to know that unique, bone-melting feeling again.

At first she hadn't the faintest idea of how to accomplish this without simply throwing herself into his arms. She could imagine his reaction to that. He wouldn't recover from the shock for days. Actually, the idea of startling Tate appealed to her, but she resisted it. Instead, she settled for a more traditional approach, a very feminine appeal. Tilting her head provocatively, she gazed unblinkingly into his eyes until she knew she had his undivided and, judging from the flush on his neck above his collar, slightly nervous attention. It turned out flirting wasn't quite as difficult as she'd thought it would be, and even without much practice her technique certainly seemed to be working fine.

"Tate," she began softly.

He cleared his throat and blinked, his brown eyes cautious. "Yes."

"Could we go someplace and dance?" She reached over and touched his hand beguilingly. "Please."

He regarded her incredulously. "You want to go to a disco?" he asked, sounding as shocked as if she'd declared a desire to have a fling in one of those adult motels with mirrors on the ceiling and king-size waterbeds.

"Of course not," Victoria replied indignantly. A disco was the last place she wanted to go. She wanted to be in the man's arms swaying to soft, romantic music, not twirling around under some blinding, flashing lights trying to find him in a crowd. "Isn't there someplace we can waltz?"

"Waltz?" His expression was bemused, as if he'd never heard the word before.

"Surely you're old enough to recall what that is. Ballroom dancing may be old-fashioned, but it hasn't vanished from the face of the earth. Can't you remember how to take a woman in your arms and move slowly around a room in time to the music?" Victoria teased.

"Of course, I remember," he retorted indignantly. "We had lessons in junior high. The boys all stood on one side of the room with sweaty palms and giggled, and the girls stood on the other side in their party dresses trying not to look desperate."

"You don't seem to remember much about the dancing part."

He shuddered. "I've blocked it from my mind."

"Well, unblock it and let's go someplace where I can prove to you that there's a very good reason for such an antiquated custom."

He paused thoughtfully, then shook his head. "I don't think there have been places like that in Cincinnati since the turn of the century."

"Of course there have. You just don't know where to find them," she charged.

"You may be right," he admitted, taking a deep breath. "Would you rather drive around and look for one or would you be willing to try my apartment instead?"

Actually, Tate thought, Victoria couldn't have given him a better opening. He'd been wondering all evening how he could entice her to come home with him so they could be alone. Blatantly suggesting that she stop by for a drink, with its implicit hint of a bedroom romp to follow, somehow bothered him. He felt as though he'd be betraying her parents' trust, which for him was an entirely new and not particularly welcome reaction. Even now, when Victoria was staring at him with come-hither eyes, he felt guilty as hell. He ought to be taking her out for a strawberry ice-cream soda, not trying to figure out how he could taste the strawberry pink of her lips in the privacy of his living room.

"That's certainly a better line than suggesting I stop by to see your etchings," she said, and he flinched as the all-too-perceptive dart struck home. But when he studied her expression more closely, he realized she actually seemed amused. She certainly didn't seem to be offended.

"Well then?" he prodded, ignoring the little voice that told him he was begging for trouble with a capital *T*.

Victoria took a deep breath. This was what she wanted, wasn't it? No man had ever made her feel quite as giddy as Tate McAndrews, and she wanted to explore that sensation, to discover what all the fuss was about. Tonight was as good a time as any. Once this tax audit was over with she might never see him again. Every true romantic deserved one wild night of explosive passion, and that was what Tate seemed to promise, if her thundering heartbeat was any indication.

"Why not?" she said boldly, ignoring the little tremor of trepidation that made her pulse lurch erratically. She also diligently silenced her ornery conscience which was reminding her that Tate McAndrews was not the right man to use for her romantic experimenting. If she happened to fall head over heels in love with him in the process, it could only lead to disaster. He was so completely unsuitable.

But he was also damnably attractive, she argued right back. Besides, she was too old to be meandering hesitantly through life as an untouched virgin. If Tate McAndrews could stir her hormones out of their pre-

viously dormant existence—and Lord knows he had—
then she'd better find out why.

When they reached Tate's apartment, Victoria's
mouth dropped open impolitely, and she stared
around her in a sort of dazed wonder. For a moment
she felt as though she were suffering from culture
shock. His furniture had absolutely no character. It
was upholstered in dull, serviceable colors, no doubt
chosen because they wouldn't show dirt if anyone had
the audacity to spill something. His paintings were
formless splashes of hideous colors hung against plain
white walls. The tables were all glass and chrome, and
not a one of them had so much as a water mark to
spoil the shiny surface. His plants were so full and
green and healthy; it seemed as though they wouldn't
dare to droop. In fact, everything was so disgustingly
tidy, so perfectly placed and so horribly sterile, Victoria was convinced he must have a filing system for
his trash. She would have given anything to find a
speck of dust anywhere or one wilting leaf on a phil-
odendron.

"Don't you ever feel like dropping your clothes on
the floor?" she asked, her expression dismayed.

Tate grinned at her, his brown eyes flashing
wickedly, as he removed his jacket with taunting deliberation. "Sure," he said softly, his gaze locking
with hers. She felt as though she'd been frozen in the
midst of a dream and couldn't wake up. The jacket fell
to the floor and her eyes followed it, widening with
disbelief. "Right now, for instance."

Suddenly her heart began drumming wildly in her
chest, and she stared up at him in confusion. "That's

not what I meant," she said, the words coming out as a choked whisper as passionate images of two nude bodies—hers and his—flickered to life in her brain. Liar, a little voice nagged. Judging from the Technicolor intensity of those images, it was exactly what she'd meant.

"Are you sure?" he taunted softly, taking a step toward her. He'd meant only to tease her, but all of a sudden the moment had turned breathlessly serious. He did want to undress, first Victoria and then himself, taking time to explore her body as she learned his. He wanted to know the feel of that creamy white skin under his fingers, to fill his hands with her breasts, to arouse the nipples into tight buds with his tongue, to feel her surrounding him with her moist femininity. He wanted her with a savage urgency that stunned him into immobility. He was afraid that if he took her in his arms, if he so much as kissed her, he wouldn't be able to stop until he knew every inch of her. And he could see from the half-frightened, half-hopeful expression in her blue eyes that she wasn't ready for that.

Victoria was shaking her head, reading the expression in Tate's eyes with unerring accuracy. But although she was telling him no, her pulse rate was definitely shouting yes, telling her to take all that he had to offer, to discover the hidden, untapped part of her own womanliness, to learn his masculine secrets. Confusing, contradictory thoughts roared through her head, warring for control of her actions.

How could her body yearn with such heated longing for someone her mind knew would be so wrong for her? Yet was he really wrong for her? He was strong, obviously dependable, sure of himself, in short the perfect balance for her zaniness. His instinctive protectiveness of her, even when he was most impatient, was certainly the stuff of romantic heroes, even though it tended to drive her crazy. Even now, she could tell that he was willing to follow her lead. He wanted her, but would take her only if she agreed, only if she came to him willingly and without reservations.

Lord knows, she had reservations. Why couldn't Tate have been someone else, someone more like herself? Then there would be no doubts at all. Even if he would unbend just a little, she thought, it would make all of this more understandable. For the first time in her life, her impulsive nature seemed to have abandoned her. With her first lover she would want much more than a fling, and with Tate that would be an absurd expectation. Even she knew better than to enter into a relationship with the hope of changing the other person. She'd heard enough accounts of marriages that had faltered because one partner suddenly realized those traits that had been merely bothersome during courtship were absolute hell to live with and that they weren't going to go away.

Suddenly it was all more than she could deal with. She wanted romance, candlelight and roses, impetuous adventures, laughter-filled days and passion-filled nights. She also wanted Tate, who promised no more than passion. She couldn't reconcile the two.

"I think I'd better go."

"Why?"

"This wasn't such a good idea."

"But we haven't danced yet," Tate said urgently, not wanting her to leave until he had at least held her in his arms. Surely he could keep himself under rigid control. He always had before. It wasn't until he had met Victoria that his control had snapped. Recently he'd found his temper flaring unexpectedly and his desires raging with such urgent abandon that it stunned him. Maybe if he burned an image of a disapproving Pete Harrison into his mind, he could regain his sense of balance, at least until he finished the audit.

"Danced?" she repeated blankly.

"You remember that quaint old custom," he teased lightly. "It's what we came here to do."

No, Victoria wanted to say. No matter what we said, we came here to make love and we both know it. But she knew she could never force those bluntly honest words past her suddenly quivering lips. Tate didn't see the tremor. He was walking to his stereo, selecting a tape and putting it on, as thought she had agreed to stay. When the soft strains of a ballad filled the air, he held out his arms. He looked so hopeful standing there that she couldn't refuse. Admit it, she chided herself, you don't even want to refuse. Her eyes locked with his, and she moved into his embrace, sighing softly just as he did when his arms closed securely around her.

The music surrounded them, drew them into its slow, provocative tempo. Victoria closed her eyes and gave herself up to the melody, to the wondrous sensation of feeling Tate's heart throbbing next to hers. She was captivated by that sure, steady beat, awed by her ability to alter it with a delicate touch of her fingers along the warm curve of his spine. Held by Tate, she knew the truly magical spell of romance for the first time and wondered again if she'd been wrong, if it could possibly work. She felt beautiful and graceful, as though she were floating on air.

"You're trying to lead," Tate murmured in her ear, the whisper of warm breath delicately tantalizing, even though his words startled her.

"I am not," she retorted indignantly, moving back to scowl up at him. He gave her an infuriating, crooked grin.

"Oh, yes, you are. What's the matter? Are you afraid I'm going to step on your toes?"

"Of course not."

"Then you don't trust me enough to follow me," he said flatly.

Victoria suddenly had a feeling he was talking about far more than dancing. "How can you say I don't trust you? I stayed here, didn't I?"

His gaze softened, and he touched a finger to her cheek, leaving behind a trail of fire and a blush of pink. "So you did. Are you sorry?"

She stared up at him solemnly. "No. I want to be here."

"In my arms?"

"In your arms."

He grinned again and her heart flipped over. "Then how about letting me lead?"

Victoria groaned. "Is your masculine ego being threatened?"

"Hardly. It's just easier if only one of us is in charge."

"Are we still talking about dancing?" Victoria asked dryly.

"I am." His expression was all innocence, though she had a feeling his comment was about as innocent as a million-dollar lawsuit.

"Are you sure you don't still have designs on straightening out my life?" she inquired edgily.

His eyes brightened, and he suddenly tilted her backward in an unexpected and breathtaking dip. "You're admitting it could do with a little reorganizing?"

"Let me up."

"First, admit it."

"I'll admit no such thing. My life is fine, Tate McAndrews!" It was impossibly difficult to say anything with conviction from this crazy angle, but she tried. He didn't seem to believe her.

"That's why you're in trouble with the IRS, why your business is haphazard at best, why your parents want to marry you off and why your house is tumbling down—because your life is under such perfect control?"

"You're being smug again."

"I am?"

"I hate it when you're smug."

"You hate it when I'm right."

"Leave me alone."

Tate put her solidly back on her feet and dropped his arms. He shrugged. "If that's what you want."

"It's what I want," she said, glaring at him defiantly, the spell broken. The man, she decided, had about as much romance in his soul as the author of a math textbook. He certainly didn't know how to pull off a seduction.

"Are you planning a dramatic exit?" he inquired, his lips twitching in a perfectly infuriating way.

"Now that you mention it, I don't think I'll give you the satisfaction." She walked to the door, turned back and gave him a haughty look of disapproval. "Good night, Mr. McAndrews," she said with prim politeness and shut the door softly behind her.

Tate stood and counted to ten. The doorbell rang. He opened it and found her standing there, her eyes flashing angrily.

"I'd like to call a cab, if you don't mind," she said stiffly.

His lips had stopped twitching and formed a full-blown, smug smile. "I'll drive you back to your car."

"That's not necessary."

"It is necessary," he said decisively, taking her arm and steering her from the apartment.

They drove across town in a silence so thick Tate felt like screaming. A few days ago that raging feeling of pure frustration would have been totally unfamiliar, but all of a sudden it was becoming a way of life. He didn't feel the least bit thrilled about it either. He had the oddest desire to shake Victoria until she agreed to shape up her life. The image of those hazardous stairs and peeling wallpaper sent shivers of fear and dismay along his spine. He had a feeling, though, she'd never admit to needing a bloody thing, least of all his help.

She was the most stubborn, infuriating woman he'd ever met, and she obviously didn't know what was good for her.

Her parents were right. She needed him in her life. The only thing wrong with that theory was the very distinct probability that she'd drive him crazy in the bargain. He gazed over at her and discovered that she was staring straight ahead, her shoulders stiff, her mouth settled into a stern line. Perversely, he wanted to kiss her until her mouth curved into a sensual, lazy, satisfied smile again. He had a feeling if he tried, though, she'd slap him . . . and rightly so.

Victoria might be even wiser than her parents on this one, he decided reluctantly. It would be better if they never saw each other again and preserved their sanity. He could send her the outcome of the audit in the mail. Ironically, the minute he admitted to himself that she was absolutely wrong for him, that it would be wise to let her vanish from his life, he wanted her more than ever.

"Where's your car?"

"Near your office."

"Where near my office?" he said with more patience than he'd ever thought he was capable of.

"I don't know. In some lot. How many parking lots can there be around there?"

Tate groaned. There were half a dozen or more. Thank God she hadn't parked in a high-rise garage. They'd be driving up and down ramps the rest of the night.

"Couldn't you think of this as an adventure?" Victoria asked plaintively.

"Afraid not," he muttered as he circled the blocks in the vicinity of the IRS offices. Fortunately, at this hour it wasn't difficult to spot a dented blue Volkswagen sitting forlornly in the middle of a virtually empty lot. It reminded him of the sad expression in Victoria's eyes.

Don't start thinking like that, McAndrews, or you'll be right back where you started, he warned himself. He managed to keep his expression stern and unforgiving as Victoria climbed out hurriedly, dashed into her car and drove away with barely a wave. It wasn't until she'd gone out of sight that he began to experience something that was totally foreign to him. Finally, he realized it was sheer, heart-wrenching loneliness. He didn't like the feeling one bit.

Seven

For the next ten days Tate suffered, agonizing over the separation from Victoria and, for the first time in his life, turning introspective. He analyzed the attraction he felt for her from every possible angle, dismissing it as sheer folly one minute, only to seize on the memory of her delightful laugh and beguiling smile the next. He was behaving in such an uncharacteristically sloppy, withdrawn way that his friends began asking first subtle, and then more pointed questions. They worried about an illness, a family problem, a financial reversal. No one seemed to suspect that a woman was involved. They all knew that Tate McAndrews would never allow a woman to disrupt his life so dramatically.

And his orderly life was most definitely being disrupted. In fact, it was in an unbelievable state of chaos. While he daydreamed, work piled up on his desk until even Pete commented on the disorganized clutter. At home he left unwashed coffee cups in the sink and clothes scattered on the floor. He didn't even seem to notice. One plant suddenly wilted and died, its bedraggled remains ignored. He opened magazines, stared uncomprehendingly at the pages and then dropped them. They stayed wherever they fell.

Only one image seemed to register fully in his mind—Victoria's. He pictured her as he'd first seen her, dangling precariously upside down from a tree branch. It was an enchanting, unforgettable image. He recalled the half-astonished, half-temptress look in her blue eyes when he'd kissed her for the first time, and his body began behaving like a teenager's, turning hot and ready at the mere memory of the way she'd felt in his arms. He was not used to having absolutely no control over his life, his thoughts or his body. Much more of this and he'd go stark raving bonkers, he thought desperately.

You can either forget her or do something, he told himself in the middle of Friday night as he tossed and turned restlessly amid a tangle of sheets. Since forgetting her seemed unlikely, he decided to accept the inevitable. He was going to have to kill this ridiculous obsession through overexposure. Every sensible bone in his body told him that spending more than a few hours with Victoria would drive him to distraction. He would be forced to acknowledge that she was absolutely wrong for him, and that would be the end of it. He could go back to doing his dishes and his work.

When the do-it-yourself home repair shop in his neighborhood opened Saturday morning, Tate was waiting. He selected lumber first, then hesitated about paint. Every conservative instinct in him shouted that he should buy white. He always bought white. It went with everything. Finally, he took a deep breath and pointed to what he considered to be an outrageous shade of blue . . . for a wall. It matched Victoria's eyes exactly. His hand shook, but he didn't back down. Since he wasn't about to leave anything to chance, he also bought a ladder, paintbrushes, rollers, turpentine and a complete assortment of nails and screws. At the checkout counter, he eyed the collection of items carefully, then went back for a hammer, a screwdriver and a saw.

"Gonna do a little work around the house?" the clerk said dryly.

"No, I'm going to build one," Tate replied grumpily, flinching at the figure that popped up on the cash register. Victoria was turning out to be a costly obsession in more ways than one. He handed over his credit card and wondered for the hundredth time if it made any sense at all for him to be doing this. Victoria wouldn't appreciate it. In fact, she was probably going to resent it and throw him and his blue paint right back out the door.

"Too bad," he muttered under his breath. "You're not doing this for Victoria. You're doing it to save your sanity."

"What's that, mister?"

"Nothing."

Once everything was loaded into his car, he headed for Victoria's, his determination mounting. He was going to fix up that place of hers so he could stop worrying about it and get her out of his system in the process. It was going to be a wonderful, satisfying weekend.

By the time he arrived in her driveway, he was whistling cheerfully, envisioning the serenity that would return to his life in a few short days. It was worth the price of a little paint and lumber and the hard work.

At first he was surprised that Victoria didn't come out of her house as soon as his car stopped, but then he decided it was better that she hadn't noticed his arrival. It gave him time to get everything unloaded before she threw a fit. By the time he'd be ready to knock on the door and surprise her, it would be too late to send him packing.

He was about to lean the ladder against the side of the house when Lancelot suddenly wove between his legs, meowing a friendly greeting. Tate tripped over the cat and tumbled forward, the ladder crashing through a window. Lancelot's howl of protest was almost as loud as Tate's.

Victoria heard the noisy crash just as she rolled over and prepared to snuggle back under the covers to finish a perfectly delightful dream about a man who knew exactly how to win her heart, a man who was nothing in the world like Tate McAndrews. She had taken the day off and promised herself a few extra hours of sleep to make up for all of the restless nights she'd had since she and Tate had parted. She'd been furious at him, but that hadn't kept her from missing him terribly, and she hated herself for even noticing his absence.

"What in heaven's name was that?" she mumbled, suddenly wide awake. She waited for another crash, but heard only screeches that clearly came from Lancelot and mutterings that reminded her of Tate's colorful carrying on when he fell through her stairs. Tate? She sat straight up in bed and listened more closely. No doubt about it. It was definitely Tate. She'd never heard such a wide vocabulary of expletives from anyone else. What on earth was he doing here at the crack of dawn on a Saturday morning? In fact, what was he doing here at all?

Wrapping a robe tightly around her, she ran to the window and peered out. The sight that greeted her was so unexpected, so ridiculously out of character, that it was all she could do to keep from laughing. Tate was lying on the ground his long legs tangled in a ladder, surrounded by scattered boards that resembled a giant's game of pick up sticks. His scowl as he tried to disengage himself was impressive and more than enough to convince her to save her laughter for later.

She ran down the stairs and threw open the door, her eyes widening in dismay as she noted the ladder protruding through the living room window. She knelt down and surveyed Tate quickly, looking for signs of blood, her hand brushing lightly over a bump on his forehead.

"Are you okay?"

"Fine," Tate said tightly.

She sat back on her heels then and regarded him quizzically, noting idly that he apparently did own one pair of jeans and that they fit like a well-worn glove. Instinctively her gaze surveyed the faded fabric, starting with its revelation of the hard muscles of his thighs, then moving upward to its taut stretch over his abdomen. She realized suddenly exactly where she was staring and blushed furiously. Fortunately, Tate didn't even seem to notice.

"Not that I'm not glad to see you, but exactly what do you think you're doing?" she said at last.

"I've come to help."

"With what? Demolishing my house?"

"No. Fixing it up," he explained, fighting to regain his sense of humor. He probably did look pretty ridiculous.

"You're off to a wonderful start," she said, glancing significantly at the shattered window. She sighed. "Tate, you really don't need to help. I thought we settled this the other night. I can do things for myself."

"I know you can," he agreed soothingly. Too soothingly. Victoria's suspicions flared to life. "I just thought maybe I could help. It'll go much faster if two of us work on it."

"Why does it matter so much to you how fast it goes?"

This was the tricky part. Tate knew he couldn't very well admit that he wanted to get her off his mind once and for all, so he settled for a half-truth. "I'm worried about your living like this. I'll feel better when you're settled."

It probably wouldn't do to analyze why he was worried about the way she lived in the first place. He just had to keep telling himself that once he stopped worrying, he would also stop thinking about her at all. He looked up, and his gaze met eyes that were filled with skepticism.

"Don't say it," he said.

"Don't say what?"

"Don't tell me again that it's none of my business how you live."

"It isn't."

"Maybe not, but I feel responsible."

"That's absurd."

He nodded. "I know it."

Suddenly Victoria grinned as she realized exactly how Tate must feel about finding himself in this position. He had probably never before done something that made as little sense as this. She could see from the confusion in his eyes that he didn't quite know what to make of it all now, either.

"As long as you're here, why don't you come on inside and have some breakfast?" she suggested.

"I have to finish unloading the car."

Victoria cringed. She couldn't afford too many more broken windows. "Leave it for now. I'll help you later."

Maybe it would be a good idea to have some coffee first, Tate decided. Not that this accident had been his fault. If that fool cat hadn't gotten in his way, Victoria would still be upstairs sleeping peacefully in her brass bed, her tousled red hair spread over the pillow, a sheet barely covering the curve of her breasts. He choked back a moan of pure frustration. He suddenly wanted, more than anything, to be in that bed with her.

Instead, he followed her docilely into the kitchen, trying not to notice the way her silk robe draped provocatively over her rounded rear. So far this was not exactly working out the way he'd intended. Instead of killing his interest, it was fanning it until he felt as though flames were shooting through his body.

"Why don't you go on and get dressed?" he suggested in a husky whisper. At her odd look, he cleared his throat and added, "I could start on breakfast, if you'll tell me what you want."

"I want everything," she said. "Breakfast on the weekend is my favorite meal. I want eggs and bacon and pancakes with maple syrup."

Tate stared at her blankly. "Umm, how about if I get the coffee started?" he offered.

Victoria grinned knowingly. "Terrific. I'll be back in a minute."

While she was gone, Tate tried not to imagine her slipping out of that robe, stepping into a hot shower and then slowly drying herself before dressing in skimpy little bikini pants and a lacy bra. He didn't succeed. He could visualize with breathtaking clarity every sensual movement. He nearly scooped the instant coffee into the pitcher of orange juice he'd found in the refrigerator. Forcing himself to concentrate, he got out the eggs, bacon and milk and set them carefully in a precise row on the counter. He found the dishes and neatly set the table. After first searching every cupboard, he finally retrieved the frying pan from the oven. He looked at the eggs and the pan, considered making an attempt to fix the eggs and shook his head.

"She wants breakfast, not a scientific experiment," he muttered and sat down to wait.

When Victoria came back into the kitchen a few minutes later, she was wearing a pair of paint-splattered cutoff jeans that barely covered her all-too-enticing bottom and a shirt that she seemed to have forgotten to button. It was tied around her middle, leaving an expanse of bare flesh that he wanted desperately to caress. He fought to focus his gaze elsewhere. It traveled to the silky curve of her neck. He wanted to touch his lips to that tender spot. His breath was coming in increasingly ragged gulps as he ripped his eyes away from that provocative sight. He told himself he should be staring out the window at the lilacs or checking out the fine job Victoria had done repairing the tiles, but he couldn't seem to move his gaze farther than the red plaid of her shirt as it fit snugly over the curve of her breast.

"I thought you were going to get dressed," he mumbled in a hoarse whisper, then could have kicked himself for virtually admitting that he was bothered by her appearance.

"I am dressed," she said, looking at him oddly.

"Barely."

"Did you want me to wear a formal gown while I work on the house?"

"No, but you could have put on...I don't know, something more...something less...."

Suddenly Victoria chuckled. "Which do you want?" she teased softly. "More or less?"

Tate glared at her. "Never mind. Wear whatever the hell you want."

"If I'm bothering you, I'll go back upstairs and change."

"You're not bothering me," he denied.

She took a step closer to him. "Are you sure?"

She smelled like a summer garden, Tate thought idly, his senses reeling. Troubled brown eyes looked up at her.

"Damn you," he muttered helplessly. "Come here."

Victoria stood perfectly still. The laughter that had filled her eyes only a moment before had died, replaced with a smoky desire. She shook her head slowly, a soft, knowing, entirely feminine smile tilting the corners of her mouth.

"You come here," she taunted.

Suddenly, with an agonized groan, Tate was out of his chair and pulling her into his arms. His lips burned against hers, demanding that they part, his tongue urgent in its quest for the tender, tentative touch of hers. His hands sought the bare skin at her waist and molded her body into his, relishing the way silk had turned to fire under his touch. Her hips instinctively tilted forward into the cradle of his, driving him nearly mad with longing. He wanted to take her right here in the middle of her kitchen. He wanted to rip that ridiculous outfit away from her body and expose every inch of flesh beneath it to his passion-sharpened gaze, to his hungry lips. He wanted to know that she was as crazy with this driving need as he was, to feel her responding to his lightest touch, crying out when the white-hot urgency of her arousal and desire matched his. He wanted.... Oh, Lord, he thought with a shuddering moan, he wanted her. He needed her.

"Victoria." Her name was uttered as half groan, half sigh as his lips burned against her neck, his tongue a moist brand that seared her. Her fingers danced through the thickness of his hair, skimmed the tight, muscled flesh of his shoulders, setting off a trembling in him that excited her beyond belief. Gone was Tate's intimidating self-control. Gone was that awesome straitlaced creature of habit, who seemed so far beyond her reach, so rigidly superhuman. This Tate was yielding, touchable and very, very human. In his arms, Victoria felt every inch a woman, a sensual, attractive woman who was all softness to his strength, all silk to his rougher denim.

Her skin was alive and tingling where his touch had branded her. Her lips burned against the hard, hair-roughened wall of his chest, and her tongue tentatively tasted flesh that was hot and damp from the fever of a passion she still couldn't quite believe. Her probing fingers, her thrusting hips, her thirsting mouth urgently sought to bring him beyond the point of denying her what she wanted so desperately. She knew instinctively that there might come a point when reason would return, when Tate's sensible nature would again seize control, and he would push her away, fighting against the pleasure they both wanted. She had to keep that from happening.

In the days they had been apart, she had made her decision. She knew that, if given another chance, she would take all that Tate had to offer for however long it lasted. She had forged a new strength to withstand any attempt he might make to change her. She believed with all her heart that she could have Tate, if she wanted him, without losing herself. If she wanted him... the words echoed distantly in her mind. Oh, yes, she wanted him, with every fiber of her being.

Her bare legs brushed against his thighs, against the hard evidence of his desire for her. She had worried that she might be a little frightened, a little tentative, when this moment finally came, but she wasn't. She was ecstatic, aggressive. Her heart was filled with so much joy, she thought she might burst, and she seemed to know exactly what to do, exactly how to excite him.

"Tate..."

"Hmmm." The low murmur barely interrupted the nearly unbearable, utterly sweet assault of his tongue on her aroused breast.

"Let's go upstairs."

"What's upstairs?" he mumbled from a daze of sensual delight.

Victoria smiled softly at his bemused state. "The bedroom."

"Bedroom?" He raised his head and his eyes widened, as though he had just realized where all of this was leading.

Sensing his slow return to sanity, Victoria stood on tiptoe and kissed him, dueling his tongue with her own, battling his sudden resistance. For a woman who'd never before seduced or been seduced—at least not successfully—she knew precisely how to work her will on him. In a matter of seconds, he was again moaning softly, holding her so tightly that her breasts crushed against his chest, her hips firmly in place against his seeking manhood. Even through two layers of clothing, hers and his, she could feel the heat, the throbbing need. There was no possible way he could pull away from her now.

Then the phone rang, and rang again, splintering the thick, passion-filled silence, shattering the moment of breathless insanity.

Eight

"The phone is *not* ringing," Tate mumbled determinedly, nibbling on Victoria's ear.

She gasped as the moist, feather-light touch sent a series of shock waves tripping along her spine. She'd never before realized that an ear was sensitive to anything more than sound. To her utter amazement and delight, it turned out that hers seemed to be a highly excitable erogenous zone. Unfortunately, it could also still enable her to hear the phone ringing.

"Yes, it is," Victoria countered, unable to keep a sigh of disappointment out of her voice. She'd been hoping to discover if her other ear was nearly as responsive as this one, and now she wouldn't find out...at least not this morning. She might be a romantic, but she could also be realistic. Tate's eyes might be glazed with passion right now, but his innate good sense was probably fluttering back to life. Passion could not stand up to a ringing phone, not after the fifth or sixth ring.

"Don't answer it," he urged, though his voice contained more hope than conviction.

Victoria gazed at him in feigned astonishment. "You actually want me to allow the phone to go on ringing? Shouldn't you be lecturing me on being responsible? It might be a problem at the shop. It could be your office. Someone might be sick. I might have won a sweepstakes. The sky might be falling."

"Or it could be your father has ESP."

She patted his hand consolingly. "If he did, he'd be offering up a prayer of thanksgiving right now. You're falling right in with his plans."

"I doubt that. Unless he's anxious to try out his shotgun." Tate muttered, running his fingers through his hair. "Oh, answer the damn thing. The ringing is getting on my nerves."

"Don't get testy. I'm sure it's not anything personal. Whoever's calling couldn't possibly know that we were about to," her voice faltered and she blushed. "Do whatever it was we were about to do."

He chuckled at her sudden confusion.

"Don't laugh at me," she grumbled, as she snatched up the receiver. "I'm not in the habit of doing this."

"Thank goodness," he said fervently, sighing and pulling her back into his arms.

Victoria scowled at him as she muttered into the phone, "Hello." She winced at her tone; it was not her most pleasant. Not that it seemed to faze her caller, who hit her with a barrage of interested questions, then didn't even pause long enough for answers. It was just as well. With Tate's fingers now doing an erotic little dance across her stomach, Victoria was swept right back into a sensual daze that excluded the world and more mundane sensations. She barely heard the questions.

"What took you so long? You weren't still asleep, were you? Were you taking a bath? Oh, never mind. I just wanted to let you know I'd be by to pick you up in ten minutes."

There was a pause, and Victoria finally realized some sort of response was expected. She murmured distractedly, "Who is this?"

"What do you mean who is this?" The voice was thick with righteous indignation. "It's Jeannie. What's the matter with you?"

"Jeannie?"

"Jeannie?" Tate echoed, his brows lifting. "I should have known."

"Hush," Victoria hissed.

"What's going on over there, Victoria Marshall? Tell the truth. Remember, this is Jeannie. Your best friend. The friend who has read your diary and knows every one of your innermost secrets." She paused for added emphasis, then added significantly, "The friend who can read your mind."

I hope not, Victoria thought, suddenly tugging her blouse closed and trying to wriggle out of Tate's grasp. It seemed indecent somehow to have him kissing her, touching her so intimately, while her best friend was on the other end of the phone. Jeannie might not yet know this particular innermost secret, but she would definitely know something very peculiar was going on.

"I'm sorry," she apologized quickly. "I was just, umm, a little preoccupied." Tate drew her right back onto his lap and brushed his lips across the swell of pale skin revealed by the plunging V neck of her still-unbuttoned blouse. Tiny sparks sizzled straight through her, all the way down to her toes and Victoria couldn't help it: she gasped and then blushed furiously.

"Victoria Ann Marshall! Is someone with you? Is that what this is all about?" Jeannie was obviously too perceptive for her own good. She sounded pleased and very smug about her guess.

"If you've got something better to do, we can forget about the fair," she offered generously with a low, significant chuckle in her voice. Victoria wanted to strangle her. Or Tate. Or maybe both of them.

"Tell her yes," Tate was saying.

"Yes." She glared at him. "I mean no. What fair?"

"Never mind. Why don't I call you tomorrow?"

"No," she repeated adamantly, ignoring Tate's dismayed groan. It was ironic that her good sense had returned long before his had. She'd never even been aware that she had any. "What fair are you talking about?"

"The crafts fair," Jeannie explained patiently. "But don't worry about it. I can handle it alone."

"No. I'll help. I promised," Victoria said stoutly, a twinge of regret evident in her voice.

"Are you sure?"

"Yes." Maybe it was better this way, she thought, though at the moment she couldn't quite convince herself of that. Even if making love with Tate would be the mistake of a lifetime, she wanted to experience it. She had this awful feeling deep down inside that if they took more time to think about it, it would never happen. They'd both realize that there was no future for two people who were so incredibly mismatched. Her head believed that. Her heart wanted like crazy to believe that her head was wrong.

"Ten minutes then?" Jeannie was saying.

Tate's relentless fingers captured a nipple and a flash fire of blazing heat tore through her. "Make it a half hour," she said breathlessly.

Tate shook his head. "Not nearly enough," he whispered, as she hung up the phone.

"That's all we have, and I'm going to spend most of it taking a bath," she said briskly, absolutely amazed that she was apparently going to go upstairs, get dressed and walk right out of this house, when what she really wanted to do was throw herself straight back into Tate's arms. She must have a screw loose, just as he—and everyone else with the possible exception of her parents—seemed to think.

"With me?" he asked hopefully.

She grinned and shook her head sadly. "Not a good idea."

"Then you'd better make it a cold shower."

"Very funny."

Tate followed her up the stairs and sat down on the edge of her bed. Strangely, Victoria didn't feel the least bit uncomfortable about having him sitting there watching her as she got her clothes together. It was as though he belonged in this room, as though he'd been doing just this for years and years...as though they were married? The unexpected and all-too-pleasant thought sent a little tingle of excitement rippling through her. It was followed by a sharp stab of disappointment. It will never happen, she told herself. Be honestly realistic for once in your life, even if it hurts like hell. Tate McAndrews might be willing to have a fling with you because you're an attractive oddity in his life, but that will be the end of it. He'll marry a member of some country club who wears a cashmere sweater set, a double strand of pearls and a tiny hat with a little veil as she struts off to spend the afternoon analyzing the stock market.

"What am I supposed to do, while you're at this crafts thing?" He sounded exactly like a kid left alone on a rainy day.

"You could come with me."

"And spend the day checking out pot holders and carved hunting decoys? No way."

"Then you can stick around and fix the window or do whatever it was you planned on doing when you came up here with all that stuff."

"I'm not sure I like the options."

"You're the one who showed up without calling first."

"I thought you wanted me to learn to be more impulsive."

"I do," she said, brushing a kiss across his lips as she passed by on her way to the bathroom. "One of the first things you learn when you do the unexpected is that it may not turn out exactly the way you expected."

Tate blinked at her uncomprehendingly. "What? How can you use those words in the same sentence like that? No wonder you never make any sense."

"I make perfect sense. You just haven't figured out how to listen to me."

Tate stared at the bathroom door, then stood up and began absentmindedly straightening out the sheets. "There's a special way I have to listen, too?" He shook his head as he fluffed the pillows and put them neatly into place. "I'll never figure this out."

"Of course you will." Victoria opened the door and poked her head out. "But you're too analytical. You need to listen with your heart."

"Right now my heart is telling me that it would give anything to be behind that door with you."

"That's not your heart. That's your hormones."

"Maybe you ought to come back in here and give me a lesson in anatomy."

"Forget it, McAndrews. I gave up being a teacher," she retorted tartly. "Buy a book."

"I don't think a book will teach me the same lessons."

"Sure it will," she said, coming back into the room in another of her long skirts, this one a soft, silky green, and a scoop-necked blouse edged with multicolored rows of embroidery. "It just won't be as much fun." She looked from him to the bed, her eyes widening in surprise. "You made the bed."

Tate shrugged. "I needed to do something with my hands, since you weren't around."

"If you get bored while I'm gone, you could do the ironing," she suggested dryly, giving him a dazzling smile as she picked up her brush and drew it through a tangle of red hair.

"I didn't drive up here to play maid for you," he grumbled.

Victoria stopped brushing her hair and turned around and faced him, her expression puzzled. "Tate, why did you really come up here?" she asked slowly.

"I told you. I wanted to help you fix this place up."

She studied him intently. "Maybe," she said thoughtfully.

"What does that mean?"

"That might be part of it, but it's certainly not all." She shook her head sadly. "You still can't admit it, can you?"

"Admit what?" His expression was thoroughly bewildered.

"That you wanted to see me."

He coughed at her outspoken, thoroughly accurate remark. "Well..."

"Why is it so difficult for you to say it? Is it because you know as well as I do that this thing that seems to be happening between us is absurd?"

"It's true," he admitted regretfully. "We're not very well suited."

"No. We're not," she agreed candidly.

"Then why do I want to go on seeing you?" He sounded so confused and forlorn, Victoria almost wanted to take him in her arms and comfort him, but she knew exactly where that would lead. Suited or not, the chemistry between them was so volatile it made dynamite seem tamer than a Fourth of July sparkler. It could flare up with a mere look, much less an intimate caress.

"Because you want to get me into bed?" she suggested, watching his reaction in the mirror.

For a minute, Tate looked absolutely horrified. Then he looked guilty. Then he grinned. "Maybe you're right."

And wouldn't it be wonderful if she were? he thought. Maybe all it would take to stop this obsession would be one simple act of passion. He gazed at Victoria and recalled exactly how he had felt when she'd been in his arms. He'd been excited, yes, but more than that he'd wanted to hold her, protect her, cherish her. He'd never felt that way about a woman before. Most of the women he knew could take perfectly good care of themselves. As much as he hated to admit it, he knew those unexpectedly protective feelings he had about Victoria wouldn't go away once they'd made love. If anything, they'd deepen until he was caught up in a tangled web of desire and caring.

"Now we're getting somewhere," Victoria was saying triumphantly, and he wanted to warn her that she didn't have the vaguest idea what she was talking about, that this wasn't nearly as simple as she wanted to believe. This was no time to be starting a serious discussion like that, though, not with Jeannie—of the big heart, rotten cash flow and even lousier timing—about to pull into the driveway at any moment.

"Looks to me like we're not getting anywhere," he retorted, trying to keep his tone lightly teasing. "You're leaving."

"But I'll be back."

"And then?"

She sighed. "And then...I don't know." She looked him squarely in the eye and added softly, "Maybe we should both do some thinking about that, while I'm gone."

When she walked out of the bedroom, Tate stared after her in disbelief. Apparently, she did understand after all. She had realized that there were a lot of unanswered questions for the two of them, and she was as confused as he was about where or how to find the answers. Somehow that tiny sign of her own struggle with all of this reassured him tremendously. Not that he had the slightest idea why, he thought with a sigh.

"Who was he?" Jeannie asked as she set out an array of ceramic pitchers and bowls in her assigned booth at the fair. The morning sun was already taking the damp chill out of the air and making the muted blues and greens of her pottery glisten with silver-gray highlights.

"Who was who?"

"Don't play games with me, Victoria Marshall. Who was the man who had you so rattled you didn't even recognize my voice when I called?"

"What makes you think there was a man there?"

Jeannie groaned. "Your tone of voice for one thing. You always get this nervous little flutter in your voice when you're feeling guilty. I noticed it first when we were seven and you were trying to convince your mother we hadn't eaten an entire box of strawberries, even though we had red juice from head to toe."

Victoria glowered at her. Jeannie had been her friend for entirely too long and knew far too much. "What would I have to feel guilty about?"

"You tell me. Maybe it has something to do with the fact that you're denying the existence of a man, when I saw an incredibly gorgeous hunk walk into your back yard with a saw in one hand, a two-by-four in the other and bare shoulders that should be outlawed in the presence of unmarried females."

She studied Victoria closely. "Have you taken up with a handyman? It's nothing to be ashamed of, you know. In fact, it's about time you stopped being so blasted choosy. You've always wanted Clark Gable, Albert Schweitzer and a knight in shining armor all rolled into one. They don't make 'em like that anymore. I'm glad you've finally decided to settle for what's out there, just like the rest of us. You'll be much happier in the long run."

Victoria burst out laughing at her friend's determined attempt to be broad-minded and encouraging in the face of what she obviously assumed to be Victoria's unexpected indiscretion. "Thanks for your vote of confidence, but I don't need it. I have no intention of *settling* for anybody. As for Tate, he is not a handyman and, even if he were, I would never be ashamed of being involved with him."

"Then you are involved," Jeannie said triumphantly. "I'm so glad. It really is about time. What's he like? He certainly is scrumptious looking. Have your parents met him? When's the wedding?"

Victoria groaned. "You're worse than my mother."

"Then she has met him?"

"Oh, she's met him all right. For years I've thought her standards were tougher than the USDA's, but she practically branded Tate with her enthusiastic seal of approval on first sight. Before you even ask, he also has my father's blessing."

"That must mean he can discuss politics and has a decent job."

"He definitely has a job," Victoria replied dryly.

Jeannie regarded her curiously. "The way you say that, it doesn't sound as if you're impressed."

"Impressed is not the issue. He works for IRS."

"Oh, my," Jeannie murmured, her voice an interesting blend of surprise and confusion. She managed to rally quickly, though, adding cheerfully, "Well, that's certainly respectable."

"Isn't it, though."

"Why do I get the feeling that I'm missing something?"

"He is auditing my taxes," Victoria admitted casually, her eyes focused carefully on the large salad bowl she'd been fiddling with for the past five minutes.

"He's what?" This time Jeannie didn't even attempt to cover her shock.

"It's ridiculous, of course," she mumbled with a wave of her hand. "Something absolutely absurd about my making a claim for a refund the agency thinks is slightly exorbitant."

Jeannie's hazel eyes widened, and the vase she was holding slid from her fingers. Victoria grabbed for it as it fell and placed it safely on a shelf in the back of the booth.

"Oh, my..." Jeannie said.

"Stop looking at me like that. I didn't do anything wrong."

"But if they're auditing you..."

"I did something stupid, not illegal. Tate says it should all be cleared up in a day or two."

"Are you sure? Do you trust him?"

Trust Tate? Victoria thought. Oddly enough, considering the rather unorthodox manner of their meeting and their short acquaintance, she did. She knew instinctively that she could trust him with her life. "I'm sure," she said confidently, then added dryly, "Just in case, though, if they cart me away to jail, you can bring me a hacksaw."

"It's not funny."

"You're telling me."

Jeannie studied her for several minutes, until Victoria thought she would scream. "What's wrong with you?" she finally demanded. "I'm not a criminal."

"I know that. I'm just trying to figure something out."

"What?"

"If he's auditing you, what's he doing in your backyard with his clothes off...?"

"Oh, for goodness' sakes," Victoria snapped indignantly. "He had his pants on."

"Whatever. He didn't look like he was checking out your financial records when I saw him."

"He wasn't. He's fixing up the house."

"He's what?" Jeannie exclaimed.

"Have you gone deaf?" Victoria muttered, her voice filled with growing irritation, even though she realized the whole thing did sound unbelievable.

"He's fixing up the house," she finally repeated.

"Is that a new government service?"

She glared at Jeannie. "No. He's worried about me. I've told him I'm perfectly capable of fixing up my own house, but he doesn't think I'm doing it fast enough."

"Ahh," Jeannie murmured, nodding with sudden understanding.

"What does that mean?"

"Clark Gable and a knight in shining armor all rolled up in one. Tell me, does this hunk have a brain?"

Victoria knew exactly where Jeannie was headed with that one. "Don't push it."

"Don't push what?" she replied innocently. "Unless I've lost every smidgen of intuition I ever had about you, you've fallen for this guy. Am I right?"

Victoria sighed. "You may be right."

Jeannie chuckled. "It's great to hear so much conviction in your voice."

"Well, it gets a bit confusing."

"I can imagine. An IRS agent doesn't sound like your type at all."

"He's not, at least not on the surface."

"But underneath?"

"Underneath there is something about him that I can't get out of my system. He drives me absolutely crazy one minute and the next I want to be in his arms. Does that make any sense?"

"Of course it does."

"It does?"

"You're in love." Jeannie was disgustingly gleeful.

"But he's so unsuitable."

"Apparently it doesn't matter."

"It should."

"Why?"

"Just because."

"Explain, Victoria Ann!"

"I've always wanted somebody who'd sweep me off my feet. Tate's at home sweeping off my porch."

"He sounds wonderful. When you're through with him, send him to my house."

"Not on your life!"

"You *are* a goner," Jeannie said delightedly. "I love it. I can hardly wait to meet him."

"You're not going to meet him," she said firmly.

"Why not?"

"I do not need another frustrated matchmaker actively plotting against me."

"Against you? Or for you?" Jeannie taunted.

"Oh, go spin your pottery wheel," Victoria retorted grumpily.

"I will," Jeannie said agreeably, smiling smugly. "I'll start on your wedding present."

Nine

By four o'clock that afternoon every muscle in Tate's body, including some he'd never even been aware he had, ached. Instead of recommending expensive equipment and aerobics classes, fitness programs ought to be pushing the regular use of paintbrushes and a routine of ladder climbing. He'd gotten more exercise in one afternoon at Victoria's than he'd had in the last ten weeks at the gym.

He had replaced every one of the remaining broken stairs. The constant bending over to perform that task probably accounted for the dull, burning pain in his lower back. He'd also found the worst of the boards in the living-room floor, ripped them up and put in new ones. He'd had to yank, then stoop, over and over again, which most likely explained the tightness across his shoulders and the steady throbbing in the constricted muscles of his thighs and calves. He had patched the cracks in the walls and put on one coat of paint, constantly stretching over his head. His arms felt as though they weighed one hundred fifty pounds each and were going to fall off.

It had taken him a while to get the knack of all this unfamiliar home repair work. But he'd tackled the assignment with his usual methodical approach and, as he stood back and surveyed the nearly finished job, he was exhausted but triumphant and more than a little proud of what he'd accomplished. He had some small inkling now of what Victoria had been talking about. There was a lot of satisfaction to be had in working with your hands. The room was actually beginning to look habitable, though he was tempted to take Victoria's perfectly ugly sofa straight to a junkyard and put it out of its misery. He had a feeling, however, that Victoria would never forgive him. She probably believed the visible stuffing and threadbare upholstery gave it character.

He stretched and groaned. Surely the human body was not meant to do the sort of awkward physical contortions all of this activity had required. He looked at a paint roller lying on the floor and scowled. No more. His body couldn't take it. He would give anything for a long, hot shower that would soothe his tight muscles.

Well, why not? If he knew Victoria, she wouldn't be home for ages, and the bathroom had been one of her early projects. It probably had plenty of steaming hot water. He went out to the car and got the change of clothes he'd brought with him. Then, with a deep sigh of anticipation, he climbed the stairs, searching for her extra towels and went into the bathroom. He turned on the faucets full force, undressed, climbed into the tub and searched for the control to turn on the shower. There wasn't one. He looked up, hunting for the shower nozzle. Nothing. He practically cried, though he had to admit he wasn't surprised. Houses this age did not have showers, and women like Victoria preferred to soak in bubble baths anyway. The image of mounds of nearly transparent, shimmering bubbles strategically placed across Victoria's body suddenly appeared in his mind. It did not do a thing to relax him. In his mind those bubbles popped slowly and steadily, revealing more and more until his own body was taut with tension.

He muttered a low curse, plopped the stopper over the drain and watched the tub fill with almost unbearably hot water. When it was high enough, he sank down in it gratefully and felt the sore achiness begin to float away. He let his mind drift, dismayed that he still couldn't get it to focus on one of his more complicated work assignments. Instead, it was filled with more taunting images of Victoria. He remembered her almost plaintive suggestion that he spend the day thinking about their relationship and what he wanted from it.

What did he want? He wanted the feeling of being vitally alive that he seemed to have discovered since meeting her. He wanted to learn to take chances, to explore life as she did with unabashed enthusiasm and excitement. Was it possible, though, to learn to do that? How could he give up a lifetime of caution and precise, carefully thought-out behavior? He had a feeling if he tried to be as impetuous as Victoria, he'd always fear that the police were only one step away. Yet that seemed better than never taking a dare. Without risks, life would certainly be safe and boring. He should know. He was coming to realize that his had become a tedious repetition of work, unsatisfying dinner dates and distant intimacy.

He grinned at the thought: distant intimacy. Now he was beginning to pair mismatched words just as Victoria did. They made sense, too. Despite the physical intimacy of his relationships, there had been a mental distance. Those women had never touched him, never captivated his heart as Victoria had. He had no idea why this was and perhaps it didn't require his understanding. Perhaps it was enough that it had happened. If one believed in a higher being controlling destiny, Tate thought, then one had to agree that in this case He had certainly worked in mysterious ways.

Suddenly he realized that the water had grown cool and the room was filled with the deepening shadows of twilight. He quickly got out of the tub, dressed in a fresh pair of jeans and a knit shirt and went downstairs. He'd made a decision while he was taking that bath, at first subconsciously and then with full awareness. Maybe later he'd attribute it to his mind becoming waterlogged, but right now it made sense. He was going to change, and he was going to start by fixing Victoria a gourmet dinner during which he could tell her all about the conclusions he'd reached about their future.

When Victoria finally got home, it was nearly seven o'clock, and she was almost surprised to find Tate still there. All day she'd been half fearing and half hoping that he'd realize how ridiculous this whole thing was and drive back home to Cincinnati where he belonged. Instead, here he was in the middle of the kitchen with flour on his nose, a recipe book open in front of him on the counter and dirty pans piled high in the sink. The place was an absolute mess. It was wonderful and amazing and horrible all at the same time.

"I know I've been encouraging you to be less orderly, but did you have to start practicing in my kitchen?" she teased. He barely looked up at her.

"Can it," he grumbled. "Don't interfere with the cook. I'm having enough trouble without your snide remarks."

"I hate to ask, but have you ever actually made a whole meal before? I had the impression that chopping carrots and peeling potatoes the other night was a first."

"It was."

"Then don't you think you should have started with something simple?"

"This was simple."

Victoria surveyed the mess disbelievingly. "Okay," she said wryly. "Then even simpler."

"Like hamburgers?"

"I was thinking more along the line of boiled eggs."

"Very funny."

Victoria leaned against the counter and gazed at him, suddenly serious. "Tate, what is this all about?"

"What does it look like? I'm fixing dinner. I figured you'd be too tired to do it."

"That's not what I mean and you know it."

He glanced over at her and shrugged. "Okay. I'm trying to prove to you that I can change, loosen up, experiment."

Victoria didn't have the heart to point out that fixing a meal was not exactly the same as flinging caution to the wind and going up in a hot air balloon. He seemed to consider it a breakthrough.

Instead, she asked simply, "Why?"

Tate returned her gaze solemnly. "Because you have more fun than I do."

Victoria chuckled. "That's probably true enough, but I had the distinct impression you didn't approve of my idea of fun."

"Well..."

"See what I mean?"

"No. What do you mean?" He glowered at her. "Are you suggesting that I can't change? I can do anything I put my mind to, Victoria Marshall. You are going to see a transformation the likes of which hasn't been seen since...since..."

"Since Count Dracula turned into a vampire?"

Brown eyes bored into her. "Hardly."

"Tate, don't you see? If you change, you won't be Tate McAndrews anymore. I can't ask you to do that for me."

"Then you admit you'd like me to change?"

"I'm not admitting anything. I'm just saying it never works, if you're changing for another person."

"I'm not. I'm doing it for me."

Victoria regarded him skeptically. "Tate, you'll never be comfortable taking life one minute at a time, the way I do. You're a planner."

"Maybe so. But isn't it possible that we might be able to compromise? Take life one *day* at a time?"

She grinned in spite of her misgivings. "That's some compromise."

"It is when you've had your entire life mapped out for the last ten years." He gazed at her, his eyes intense and filled with an intriguing blend of hope and desire. "Give me some time, Victoria. Please. Help me to know if there can be more to my life than auditing tax returns and going to the gym."

She shook her head. "Tate, I'm sure your life has more to it than that. You love your work and you've had fun in the past. You've certainly had other relationships, haven't you, relationships that made a whole lot more sense than this one ever could?"

"That's exactly my point. They've all made perfect sense. I've been with people like me, people so caught up in their careers and in doing the right thing that they don't take any chances. I've taken more chances today than I ever have in my life. It was wonderful."

Victoria's eyes widened. "Chances? Here?" she asked anxiously. "Tate, what have you done? You didn't break any more windows, did you?"

"Of course not," he huffed. "Just wait until you see."

Victoria wasn't sure she had enough insurance to cover the possibilities or the stamina to withstand the shock. Still, she said bravely, "Let's go."

He shook his head. "Not now. After dinner, I'll take you on a tour."

"Don't you think you're being awfully optimistic?"

"What's that supposed to mean?"

"Do you actually think you're going to get a dinner out of this mess?"

"Just you wait, Victoria Marshall. You're going to regret making fun of me."

"I wasn't making fun of you. I was trying to be realistic."

"That has to be a first."

"Don't be snide. Where would you like me to sit?"

Like a maître d' Tate pulled out her chair, seated her and whipped open her napkin with an exaggerated flourish. He had just poured her a glass of wine, when the buzzer on the oven went off. Victoria's brows shot up. She hadn't even given him credit for being able to find the timer, much less knowing how to use it.

"Oh, dear," he muttered.

"What's wrong?"

"It's ready too soon. I haven't tossed the salad."

"We don't need a salad," Victoria soothed.

"Are you sure?"

"I'm sure."

"Okay," he said, relief evident in his voice. He opened the oven door and peered inside, his brow puckered in dismay.

"Now what's wrong?"

"It looks funny."

"What looks funny?"

"The soufflé."

"You made a soufflé?" Victoria couldn't keep the amazement out of her voice.

"Well, I thought I had, but it doesn't look like any soufflé I've ever seen."

"Let's see it."

With obvious reluctance Tate withdrew the casserole from the oven. Victoria eyed it curiously. There certainly wasn't any sign of a puffy golden top peeking over the rim of the dish. He walked over to the table and held it out.

"Does it need to cook some more?"

Victoria peered into the bowl and fought back the urge to giggle hysterically. It looked like a Florida sinkhole. The sides were barely three inches high and one shade beyond golden brown. The middle had simply caved in.

"I don't think baking will help it."

"Why not?"

"It's past help."

"But I've been checking it every few minutes. It seemed to be doing just fine."

Victoria's lips started twitching, and she gazed at Tate with blue eyes that sparkled with barely suppressed laughter. "You checked it every few minutes?" she said, her voice catching. "Were you careful not to slam the oven door?"

"What does that have to do with anything?"

"Tate, soufflés are very delicate. They can fall. Yours has taken a tumble."

"But I wanted it to be perfect."

"I'm sure it will taste fine," she said, though her voice lacked conviction. A moment later, with Tate gazing at her hopefully, she took a small bite, followed by a large gulp of wine.

"What's wrong with it?"

"Nothing," she denied. "It's a little hot."

"Of course it's hot. It just came out of the oven."

"That's not what I mean. Did you by any chance put any extra spices in it?"

"Extra spices?" He stared at her blankly. "No. I couldn't find the pepper shaker, so I used some of that red pepper instead, but that's all."

"Oh, my Lord," Victoria murmured.

"What?"

"Just taste it."

Tate scooped up a forkful, swallowed it and grabbed for his wineglass. His eyes watered.

"It's awful."

"Not awful exactly. Just spicy."

"We can't eat this. I'll make sandwiches."

Victoria stood up hurriedly. "No. You stay where you are. You've done enough. I'll make the sandwiches."

Tate grinned. "You don't trust me, do you?"

"Well, you did put hot pepper in a spinach soufflé."

"I wouldn't put it on the sandwiches."

"Maybe not, but humor me."

"Maybe we should take a look at the house first."

"Think that'll kill my appetite completely?"

Tate glared at her. "You're going to be sorry you said that."

"I hope so," Victoria muttered under her breath as she started toward the door.

"What did you say?"

She gave him a dazzling smile. "I said I can hardly wait."

Tate's tour started on the porch, where he pointed out the window he'd replaced. Then he showed her the stairs, all now solid-looking and even.

"I'm impressed," she admitted.

"Wait," he said, his brown eyes sparkling with an excitement that made her heart flip over. "Close your eyes."

"I won't be able to see if I close my eyes."

"Don't worry. I'll let you open them again. I just want you to experience the full effect all at once."

A nervous edginess crept into Victoria's voice. It was interesting that as Tate had grown more impulsive, she seemed to be growing increasingly cautious. "The full effect of what?"

"Close your eyes and come with me," Tate insisted, taking her hand. "Are they closed? They don't look closed."

"Tate, if I close them any tighter, I'll get wrinkles."

"They'll add character."

"I don't want character."

"Humph!"

Victoria noted that the hand clutching hers so tightly was much rougher than the hand that had caressed her that morning. For a moment she felt almost guilty about going off and leaving Tate alone to do all of this work. Then she visualized the mess in the kitchen and thought about how long it was likely to take her to repair the damage. Her guilt vanished. She'd say they were about even so far.

Suddenly they stopped and Victoria's nose twitched. Paint? She smelled paint. Suddenly she had this horrible vision of dull white walls. She'd known the minute she walked into his apartment that Tate's imagination did not stretch beyond white.

"Open your eyes," he said excitedly.

She took a deep breath and tried to prepare a properly enthusiastic response. After all, the man deserved some credit for trying. She opened her eyes. She rotated around in a tiny circle. Her brows rose ever so slightly. Her mouth dropped open.

"Tate, it's . . ."

"Do you like it?" he asked anxiously.

"It's so . . . blue."

"I thought it matched your eyes."

In that instant, with those softly spoken words, the room went from mere blue to incredible, spectacular and a dozen other adjectives it took to adequately describe the joy that shot through Victoria's heart. He'd bought the paint to match her eyes. If that wasn't the sweetest, most unexpected, most . . . romantic thing to do. She stood on tiptoe and threw her arms around him.

"Oh, Tate," she said, her eyes shining and turning a deeper, more intense blue than Tate had ever seen before. "It's the most beautiful room I have ever seen."

He knew then that every backbreaking moment had been worth it. The thrill of pleasing her, of surprising her was like no other emotion he'd ever experienced.

He would climb mountains or tumble out of airplanes to keep that look on her face. Instead, he kissed her, his tongue flickering gently across her lips, teasing them into parting, urgently seeking her nectar, the uniquely sweet taste that was all Victoria.

With innocent abandon, she sighed and yielded to his embrace, like a child curling sleepily into the arms of a parent. But there was nothing childlike about her response in that moment of surrender. She was all woman in his arms, her body quivering under his deft touch as it roved over warm shoulders, curving spine, rounded buttocks and firm thighs. He felt the heat rising through her, matching his, blending with it until an urgent, white-hot fire raged between them.

Her hands were questing over his body, rippling along his muscles that were thirsting for her touch, tensed from the waiting, coiled even tighter when it came. They needed the release only she could bring. They needed to experience those delicate hands kneading, teasing, tempting him. He groaned aloud as her hand skimmed tentatively across the front of his jeans.

"No, babe," he pleaded. "Not yet." His control could take only so much.

"Tate, please don't stop," she pleaded. "I want you to love me."

"But we need to talk, remember. We need to think about what we want."

"I know what I want. I want to feel you inside me. I . . . I've never felt like this before, and I want it to be with you."

A thrill of pleasure soared through Tate, then hesitated and drifted down, turning into doubt. Could she possibly know what she was saying? Was she really willing to give her greatest gift to him? After all, she still thought they were mismatched and deep down so did he. Nothing had happened to change that and making love would only confuse the issue.

She lifted his hand and placed it over her breast. He could feel the nipple harden. She gazed up at him, and there was a mute appeal in her eyes, an appeal it was taking every ounce of willpower he possessed to deny.

"Please," she whispered. "Please."

Tate buried his face in her hair, the golden-red curls surrounding him with fragrant silk. His body shuddered.

"Tate?"

"God help me, I want you too much to say no," he told her, scooping her into his arms and carrying her up the stairs. "We'll just have to sort it all out later."

When they reached the bedroom he carefully set Victoria on her feet, as though she were the fragile doll she'd once reminded him of. Then he turned down the covers on her brass bed, each hurried movement giving him a startling sense of déjà vu because he'd envisioned it so often in the last few days. She started to take off her blouse, but he stilled her hands.

"No," he said softly. "I want to do it."

Victoria saw the heated look of desire in his eyes and trembled. She had wanted this moment, wanted him so much and now it was happening. Her flesh burned, where his knuckles grazed it as he lifted her blouse over her head. His kisses fluttered across her shoulders, moist heat that seared soft satin. Her bra was unhooked and fell away and his lips replaced the lacy fabric, caressing, at first tenderly and then with an urgency that filled her breasts with an aching tautness. Waves of pleasure reached in and down, spiraling through her to some secret center of excitement that she'd never before realized she possessed.

Without her even knowing that Tate had touched it, her skirt slid to the floor, and her legs, which logic told her should have been cooled by the evening breeze, burned with an inner heat.

"You are so beautiful," he murmured softly, as his sure fingers skimmed over her anxious flesh, along the silken curve of her waist, over narrow hips and along firm thighs, drawn inevitably toward that trembling warmth between her legs. When his palm cupped her, Victoria gasped with surprise and delight. She'd had no idea what a man's touch would feel like there, no idea that it could create this breathless flutter of anticipation that was building into a thrill of tension that threatened to overtake her and send her senses reeling out of control.

"You're ready, aren't you?" She was so lost in the sensations flowing through her that Tate's voice seemed to come to her from a great distance.

Ready? She felt as though she'd been ready for a lifetime, waiting for this. "Yes," she murmured. "Oh, yes, Tate, I'm ready. I want you."

He slipped her pants off and then placed her gently on the bed. Victoria felt bereft without him, the fires inside were cooling, but as Tate yanked his shirt over his head, revealing his well-muscled chest with its scattering of crisply curling brown hairs, the flames built again. Victoria's fascinated eyes followed the movement of his hands as he unsnapped and then unzipped his jeans and slid them slowly down over lean hips, taking his briefs with them. Her breath caught in her throat at her first sight of him fully aroused for her. He was so utterly masculine, so incredibly virile. He was magnificent! She held out her arms to him and he came to her.

When flesh met flesh, Victoria's body responded with an urgency and eagerness that she could see from the look in Tate's eyes . His hands moved slowly over her, taunting her. Her body twisted and turned, alive with a yearning need to know it all, to feel the ultimate union of two highly different individuals into a uniquely special whole.

"Now, Tate, please," she pleaded.

"Shhh. I want to be sure you're ready," he soothed, his fingers gliding over the intense peak in which her arousal seemed to be centered to touch even warmer flesh. "I don't want to hurt you."

"You won't," she murmured softly against his chest, her lips moist and seeking, searching for a masculine nipple to feel the satisfying tension that could be aroused by a gentle flick of her tongue. "Nothing you could do could ever hurt me."

Tate knelt over her, poised, his eyes gazing down at her with love and desire and tenderness. Instinctively, Victoria's hips lifted to meet him, and the touch of that moistness lured him inside with a slow, steady thrust that hesitated only once, when a tiny cry escaped her lips.

"No, please," she said urgently, her hands on his hips drawing him to her, refusing to allow the retreat.

And then, once that instantaneous, tiny shock of pain was gone, she was filled with new waves of excitement that built to an incredible peak, calling to her, luring her to a place of awesome beauty and previously unimagined adventures. Suddenly she realized it was Tate's voice she heard, Tate calling out her name, as his body shuddered in an extraordinary moment of released passion, taking her with him on the most thrilling, romantic journey of all.

Ten

―――――

As Victoria came slowly and reluctantly awake, she sensed that someone was staring intently at her. After awakening alone for twenty-eight years of her life, it was a most disconcerting feeling. It also felt wonderful to realize that Tate was next to her, and that it was his body causing that dip in the mattress, causing her to roll to his side. Smiling softly, she stretched and turned toward him, wanting to feel his arms around her again.

"Morning," she murmured quietly, not wanting to shatter the pleasant early morning hush of daybreak. She opened her eyes to meet his steady gaze, but as she took in the look of dismay on his face, her own gaze wavered. "What's wrong?"

"How could I do it? How could I be so stupid?"

"Do what?" She shook her head to try to clear the cobwebs. "Tate, I am not very good in the morning. You're going to have to try harder to make sense."

"How could I make love to you without protecting you?" he muttered, burying his face in his hands. If the eyes were the windows to the soul, Victoria thought, then Tate's soul was deeply troubled.

"You were a virgin, damn it. I never should have touched you. What if you get pregnant?" he said, then added decisively, "I'll marry you. That's all there is to it. We may have some problems adjusting at first, but we'll work it out. We ought to start thinking about a date."

"Tate . . ."

His head snapped up. "What?"

"Don't worry about it."

"What do you mean don't worry about it? Of course I'm going to worry. I've never done anything this foolish and irresponsible before in my life. I never wanted to hurt you, and now I might have gone and gotten you pregnant. My God!"

"Tate, it's okay," she said soothingly, putting her cool hand on his bare shoulder. The flesh was warm, inviting. She felt him tremble, right before he decisively shrugged off her touch. He groaned aloud.

"Touching is not a good idea. That's what got us into this mess."

"Tate McAndrews, I will not have you describing the most beautiful night of my life as a mess!" Victoria snapped.

"Tell me that a few weeks from now when you're pregnant."

"I am not going to get pregnant."

"Do you have some sort of exclusive on luck?"

"No," she said patiently. "But I took care of it. I saw a doctor...right after we met." She blushed. "Well, not exactly right after, but soon...I mean once I knew...."

He gazed at her as though she'd announced that she'd been praying to a fertility god. "You..."

"Saw a doctor," she repeated firmly. She grinned at him, noting the relief in his eyes. "Someone had to be sensible," she added with a shrug.

Laughter bubbled up then, and Tate pulled her back into his arms. "You are incredible, Victoria Marshall."

"I've always thought so. I'm glad you've finally figured it out," she said, gasping when he nipped playfully at the taut peak of her breast. "Tate!"

"Yes," he said innocently.

"What time is it?"

"I'm trying to make love to you, and you want to know what time it is?"

"I'm due at an auction at ten. I don't want to be late."

Tate moaned. "The woman who has never once in the two weeks I've known her been on time is worried about not being late to an auction. I can't decide whether to be astonished or insulted."

"Go for astonished. It's easier on the ego," she said as she rolled over top of him to see the clock for herself. "Whoops. It's nearly nine. I've got to get moving."

"You move much more, wiggle even one tiny finger, and you won't get out of this bed for a week," Tate announced in a voice so filled with urgency that Victoria froze.

"How do you expect me to get out of bed if I can't move?" she asked breathlessly, as her body became instantly aware of exactly how many interesting points of contact it had established with Tate's.

"I am going to do the moving. I am going to lift you ever so slowly so that you do not rub against me," he muttered, a low growl in his voice.

She wiggled.

"Victoria!"

She wiggled again and grinned. "Maybe I could be just a little late."

They arrived at the auction at noon. The yard of the farmhouse was crowded with familiar faces and the auctioneer's voice was filling the air with the rat-a-tat-tat patter that kept the bidding moving at a head-spinning pace. An excitement built inside Victoria, almost as great as that she'd experienced in Tate's arms. She loved exploring the rows of furniture and cartons of household goods at a farm sale, looking for some special treasure. Sometimes it seemed the more battered and decrepit the item, the more it appealed to her sense of discovery. She always wanted to learn what was under the paint or beneath the rust. Then she tried to imagine the lives it had touched. Maybe that was what made antiques so special to her, the fact they each had a history, stories they could tell about someone who had treasured them.

Because they were late, she didn't have time to do her usual advance survey of the items being offered. She signed up for a number so she could bid, then pulled Tate through the crowd.

"I'm starved," he murmured in her ear. "Can't we get something to eat?"

"You can. I'm working."

Tate's sharp gaze swept over the scene. "Are all of these people working?"

Victoria regarded him quizzically. "Tate, haven't you ever been to an auction before?"

"Never."

She shook head. "That's what happens when you spend your life playing games with rows of boring numbers. You miss all the fun."

"I thought you said this was work."

"It is for me. But a lot of these people just like to come and spend the day visiting with their friends. It's sort of like an old-fashioned community picnic."

His eyes lit up. "Picnic?"

Victoria grinned at his hopeful expression. "There are tables of food right over there. Go get something, if you're hungry."

He nodded and loped off through the crowd. When he returned a few minutes later he was carrying two plates piled high with hot dogs, homemade potato salad, coleslaw and slices of both cherry and apple pie. Victoria's eyes widened incredulously.

"I didn't want anything," she told him.

"Good," he said, grinning at her. "This was all for me. We never did have dinner last night, and you made me skip breakfast."

"We would have had time for breakfast, if you hadn't . . ." Her voice trailed off.

"Hadn't what?" he teased.

"Tate, please. You're distracting me."

"Am I?" he asked innocently. "Good."

"It is not good. I have to pay attention."

While Tate ate, Victoria studied the crowd, trying to pinpoint who the heavy bidders were and what they were buying. Only a handful seemed to be dealers or serious collectors. The rest were the usual assortment of auction followers, who bid erratically and frequently too high simply because an item appealed to them. Their unpredictability was what gave the auction its challenge. You had to know the value of every piece and set your limits, or you could be lured into a bidding war with someone to whom price was no object.

Tate watched with amazement as the intensity in Victoria's eyes mounted and her brow puckered into a tiny, fascinating frown. Somehow he'd thought of her business as a game, primarily because of her unique way of conducting it. He saw now that it was anything but a game to her. She took it seriously and, judging from the careful way she was watching the crowd, she knew what she was doing. Apparently she had to be as good a judge of people as she was of antiques.

He had been paying so much attention to Victoria that he'd lost track of what was happening on the makeshift stage set up under a huge oak tree. When she lifted the number she'd been holding in her lap, his gaze flew to the stage to see what she was trying to buy.

It looked like a huge stack of unmatched dishes to him, and they were all in these glaringly bright shades of orange and red and blue. He couldn't imagine eating food off plates those colors.

"You're kidding!" he muttered aloud. "You want those things?"

"It's Fiestaware," Victoria said excitedly, as if that explained everything.

"Oh," he said and looked again. "It doesn't match."

"It doesn't have to," she said and flashed her card again. "Many collectors want a mix of colors. Others are looking for a single piece to fill in a set. I like to get as much as I can find."

The bidding had intensified, with only Victoria and two others remaining. Her card was waving in the air more frequently than a flash card at a high-scoring football game. Tate could barely tell from the auctioneer's rapid chatter exactly what the current price was, but it sounded outrageous to him. One of the remaining bidders dropped out, leaving only two. It was up to Victoria. She hesitated, then waved her card.

The other bidder promptly raised her offer and Victoria's face fell in disappointment. When the auctioneer looked back at her, she shook her head.

"You're going to drop out now?" Tate asked incredulously, as the auctioneer began his chant, "Going! Going! . . ."

Tate snatched Victoria's card and held it in the air.

"Tate, what are you doing?"

"You want it, you're going to have it," he said adamantly.

Victoria tried to snatch the card back. Tate held her hand up. When his bid was raised, he managed to wrestle the card away from Victoria long enough to wave it in the air. By now people around them were chuckling, but he didn't care. All he knew was that Victoria was going to have those dishes if it was the last thing he did.

"Tate McAndrews, stop it this minute," Victoria pleaded. "I can't afford to go any higher."

"I'll pay for the dishes."

"Tate," she said, his name coming out as a soft groan. "Please."

"You want them," he repeated insistently.

"Not for me."

His eyes flew open, and the card drifted back to his lap. "Not for you?"

"No. For the shop. I'm going to sell them."

"Oh. Of course," he said quietly, as the auctioneer said with a broad grin, "Sold to the gentleman... and lady...in the fifth row."

"Oh," Tate repeated, and this time his eyes were wide with shock. Victoria's lips were suddenly quivering, and then she was laughing, unable to control her mirth.

"Tate, you were wonderful."

"I feel like a fool."

"No," she said, kissing him. "You did something impetuous, totally crazy, absolutely impulsive, just to make me happy. I love you for it."

"You do?"

"I do," she said, grinning at him.

He chuckled and winked at her. "Should I do it again?"

"Don't you dare. We'll both go broke."

As the spring days lengthened toward a summery brightness, Tate spent more and more time with Victoria. They managed to avoid her inquisitive parents and an enthusiastically watchful Jeannie, though that was getting to be an uphill battle. One night, Victoria fully expected one of them to pop out of her closet just as she and Tate were rediscovering the magic that their bodies made together.

Though Victoria had tried to force Tate to include her in his life in Cincinnati, he'd been more insistent that he wanted to understand hers first. If he had told her once, he had told her a thousand times that he wanted to experience firsthand the lightheartedness that made her lips curve in a perpetual smile and her eyes sparkle like jewels in sunshine. When he said such uncharacteristically romantic things with a serious gleam in his eyes, her heart flipped over. She found herself doing exactly what she'd sworn not to. She fell more and more deeply in love.

Unfortunately, on top of that, none of her attempts to bring a sort of innocent pleasure, a more casual abandon into Tate's too-structured life went exactly according to plan. It was as though the same fate that had willfully thrown them together to fall in love had now decreed that it couldn't possibly work.

First, she had arrived at Tate's office in the middle of the day and dragged him on a picnic. It had gone beautifully once he'd stopped grumbling about the disruption in his busy schedule. She'd prepared a lovely lunch, brought along a book of poetry and found an idyllic setting. After they'd eaten, she'd leaned against a tree with Tate's head nestled in her lap, and started to read to him, her melodious voice filling the air with softly spoken, romantic words. It had been just about perfect...until a bee had settled on Tate's lip. She could still hear his startled shout, and she would never forget the frantic trip to the emergency room, once his lip had started swelling to at least three times its normal size.

"I'm sorry," she had said over and over again.

"No' yo' fau'," Tate mumbled thickly.

"Yes, it was. If I'd had any idea you were allergic to bees, I would have..."

"Wha'?"

"I don't know. I could have done something." She'd run her finger lightly across his lip and winced as she saw a flicker of pain in his eyes. "Oh, Tate."

"Shhh," he had said soothingly. "Don' worry abou' i'."

But she had worried and a few days later, when Tate had insisted on helping her plant her vegetable garden, she had practically pitched a fit, imagining him attacked by a whole swarm of bees and blowing up to the size of a hot air balloon.

"Victoria," he'd said patiently. "I'm sure the odds against my being stung again are a million to one."

"They are if you stay indoors."

"I'm helping with the garden." She knew that tone by now. She swallowed her doubts and gave him a shovel.

They had pulled weeds and cleared the patch of ground in the side yard, worked the rich black soil until it was absolutely perfect, added organic fertilizer and then put in rows of tiny tomato, corn and green bean plants.

"Where's the watermelon?" Tate had asked.

"I hate watermelon."

"I don't."

They had driven back to the garden store, where he had picked out three watermelon plants.

"Tate, one would be enough."

"What if it died?"

"Okay. Then two should do it."

"You might decide you like it."

Victoria had sighed. "Get three if you want them."

By the time she'd relented, he'd already paid for them. The man was completely stubborn.

It wasn't until later that night that they discovered the garden had been filled with poison ivy. For some unknown reason only Tate got a reaction to it. His arms were covered with a bright pink rash that he kept scratching until Victoria threatened to bandage his hands with adhesive tape.

"Tate, don't you think maybe we ought to do something in Cincinnati this weekend?" Victoria had suggested the previous night. "Maybe we could go to a movie."

"What would you do if you weren't with me?"

She'd shrugged. "I don't know. I never know exactly what I'm going to do until I'm practically in the middle of it."

"Well, if the weather's nice what would you probably do?"

"Go fishing, I suppose."

Tate had regarded her with a pained expression. "Fishing?"

"Sure."

"But what do you do while you're waiting for the fish to bite?"

"You don't *do* anything. It's so peaceful just to sit on the edge of the river and dangle your feet in the cold water and feel the sun touch your face. The sun feels almost as good as you do," she'd murmured, curving herself into his eagerly receptive body.

That had brought an abrupt halt to the discussion for the moment, but this morning she'd awakened to the sight of Tate standing by the bed with a sheepish expression on his face, a fishing pole in his hands and a hook caught in the seat of his jeans.

"Don't say it," he'd muttered, as she barely stifled a grin. "Just get it out."

After that she'd finally convinced him that they should drive to Cincinnati for a concert. It had taken them an hour to decide between a world famous violinist and an outrageous punk rock star with spiked pink hair and more mascara on his eyes than Victoria had ever worn in her life.

"But we both love classical music," Tate had argued. "Why would you even suggest we go to see this other jerk?"

"Have you ever seen a punk rock group?"

"No."

"Well, neither have I. It's time we did."

"Give me one good reason."

"It's an experience."

Tate couldn't find a single argument that could stand up to that kind of logic. "I'll call for tickets."

They never got to the concert, for which Tate would always be eternally grateful. They were on their way, in fact they were only a few miles away, when Victoria spotted a carnival.

"Oh, Tate we have to stop."

"We do?"

"Carnivals are such fun."

"No, they're not. They're grubby and cheap and disgusting."

"Tate, please."

"Oh, to hell with it." He couldn't resist it when she turned those blue eyes of hers on him with such a wide-eyed look of innocent entreaty. He vaguely understood now how men had been moved to conquer entire civilizations by the mere lift of some beguiling woman's brow. He was as helpless to refuse Victoria's wishes as a moth was to elude a flame. She was beaming at him now with that dazzling smile that warmed his heart and turned his determinedly rational head to absolute mush.

He parked the car, and they strolled hand in hand through the dusty lot onto the fairway. Raucous, tinny music filled the air with a cheerful noise. A Ferris wheel, decorated with bright lights, spun through the early evening sky, its stark reds and greens and blues streaking through the muted mauves of twilight. The distinctive scents of sticky, sweet cotton candy, fresh popcorn, garlicky sausage, hot dogs and pizza blended together to create a mouth watering effect. Barkers were trying to lure the crowd to try its luck pitching pennies, throwing hoops around milk bottles or shooting a moving target of tiny wooden ducks. Tate thought the whole thing had an air of awful unreality about it, but Victoria's expression was alive and excited, her eyes sparkling.

She drew him first to the cotton candy booth.

"You're not really planning to eat that stuff?" Tate asked, horrified by the puff of blue that was twirling around a paper cone.

"We're going to eat it," Victoria replied firmly, as he reluctantly paid for the candy. She pulled off a chunk and tried to feed it to him.

"That's nothing—" his protest began, as she poked some of the sticky blue mess in.

"—but sugar," he concluded, deciding it wasn't too awful. But it certainly had no nutritional content. "What a waste of calories."

"We didn't come here to diet. We came here to have a good time."

"And eating blue stuff is a good time?"

"Yes."

"If you say so," he said doubtfully. "What are we doing next for fun?"

"The Ferris wheel."

Tate's eyes surveyed the spinning wheel skeptically. "I don't think so. Those things aren't safe."

"Of course they are. How often have you read about one breaking?"

"Once would be enough, if you happened to be on it."

"Tate, it won't collapse."

"Do you have an in with the mechanic?"

"Buy the tickets."

"You want me to contribute to my own death? That's suicide."

"It's going to be murder, if you don't try to get into the spirit of this."

They were only stuck on top for forty-five minutes. Tate swore he would get even with Victoria, if it took him a lifetime.

"That's promising," she said, giving him a broad grin.

"It is? I didn't mean it to be."

"You're planning to spend a lifetime with me. Isn't that what you said?"

"Yes, but yours may end the minute we get back on the ground."

"Oh," she said softly, studying him quizzically. "Aren't you having a good time really?"

Actually, Tate supposed it wasn't the worst time he'd ever had in his life. Having the mumps at twenty-five had been pretty terrible, and having some idiot driver smash into the back of his new car twenty minutes after he drove it off the lot hadn't been too terrific. But this was definitely right up there among the top ten. He wasn't sure he ought to say that to Victoria, though. She was already upset enough about the bee and the poison ivy and the fish hook.

"I'm sure I'll have a great time once we're back down on the ground," he said with forced cheer.

"Right. We'll try the baseball toss, and you can win one of those huge teddy bears for me. I've always wanted someone to do that," she said wistfully.

At that moment Tate would have been willing to spend his next six lifetimes throwing baseballs until her entire house overflowed with those awful, ugly bears, if that was what she wanted.

His first three tosses were right on the mark, and Victoria's face was alight with laughter when the fat panda with the bright green bow around its neck was handed to her.

"Does he need a friend?" Tate asked.

"Of course," Victoria said solemnly. "Everyone needs a friend."

This time on the third toss, Tate wrenched his back and grimaced with pain.

"Tate, what is it?"

"Nothing."

"Tate, it is too something. You're holding your breath."

"Only so I won't scream."

"You hurt your back," Victoria guessed.

"It's nothing," he insisted. "I'm sorry about the bear."

"Don't worry about it. This one will be just fine. Lancelot will keep him company."

Tate suspected Lancelot would tear him to shreds, but he didn't want to put a damper on Victoria's enthusiasm.

"Is there anything else you wanted to do?"

"Let's see the fortune-teller."

"You're kidding!" Tate was incredulous. "You don't actually believe in that stuff?"

"Of course not, but it's fun."

"Just like the Ferris wheel."

"Don't be mean."

"Sorry."

They sat down in front of a woman with a yellow bandanna on her dark curls, golden hoops in her ears and red lipstick in a shade just this side of scandalous. She had dark, Gypsy eyes that told seductive tales and a contradictory, impish smile that teased like a child with a feather. Even Tate wanted to trust her. She spread the cards on the table, studied them intently, then hastily gathered them up. Her fingers moved so quickly that Tate wasn't even aware that her actions were peculiar until he heard Victoria's sharp intake of breath.

"What's wrong?" she asked hesitantly.

"Nothing," the woman said, though her tone was far from reassuring. "I made a mistake with the cards. I wish to try again."

"You saw something in the cards, didn't you?" Victoria insisted. "Tell me."

Tate reached over and took Victoria's hand. "Sweetheart, you said yourself it's only a game. Don't worry about it."

"It's not a game. She saw something, and I want to know what."

"I saw a tall, dark-haired, handsome man in your life."

"Brilliant," Tate muttered. The woman and Victoria glared at him.

"It was all wrong. It will never work out," she said, as Victoria's eyes filled with tears.

"I knew it," she murmured, looking at Tate. "I just knew it."

Tate wanted to throttle the woman. "Are you out of your mind? Can't you see you're upsetting her?"

"I only say what I see in the cards."

"Tate, I've always known it wouldn't work. We've been pretending, trying to turn a dream into reality."

Tate stared at her incredulously. "Victoria, this is the most ridiculous conversation I have ever had in my life. Are you trying to tell me that you're willing to let some crazy fortune-teller dictate what happens to us?"

"Sir, I am not crazy!"

"Oh, be quiet," Tate snapped. "You've done enough damage."

"I want to go home," Victoria said quietly.

"Victoria, please."

"I want to go home."

"Of all the simpleminded, ridiculous—"

"Now I'm simpleminded and ridiculous?"

Tate's head was reeling. "I don't believe this."

"Neither do I. I thought you were starting to love me a little bit, but you were just treating me like some circus freak show, weren't you?"

"What? Where the hell did that come from?"

"You've always thought I was just some dingy kook. Admit it."

"I thought you were unique, unusual, charming and wonderful. I do love you."

"You think that now, but when the novelty's worn off, you'll go right back to some prissy little career woman who buys her clothes in New York or Paris or someplace, instead of a secondhand store."

"Victoria, I don't give a damn where you buy your clothes."

"That's not the point."

"What is the point? I haven't been able to figure it out since we sat down at this stupid booth."

"We're all wrong for each other. Look at the last few weeks. You've tried. You really have tried, but you haven't had fun. Good heavens, you've been practically killed by a bee."

"Oh, for heaven's sakes," he said, rolling his eyes in disgust. "I was not practically killed."

"Whatever. And you got poison ivy. And you got a fish hook stuck in your rear. And you hurt your back tonight. If you keep trying to be more like me, you'll end up dead."

Tate sighed. He had a feeling there was no point in arguing with Victoria when she was in this state of mind. Maybe by the time they drove home, she'd be seeing things more rationally.

Or maybe by then, he'd at least figure out what the devil she was talking about.

Eleven

Victoria had heard the crazy, irrational words pouring out of her mouth and wanted to stop them, but she couldn't bring herself to be silent any longer. Deep down, she really believed what she had said: she and Tate were absolutely wrong for each other. The idea was hardly a new one. It had nagged at her from the very beginning, and their ill-fated attempt to make the relationship work had given her proof. The phony fortune-teller finally made her admit aloud to Tate and forced them both to face what they should have known from the start.

The last few weeks had been their impossible dream. In many ways she had been happier than she'd ever been in her life. She'd never laughed harder or shared more tender moments. Certainly she had never experienced any greater heights of passion. Tate had tried so hard to please her and ultimately, that was the problem. He had needed to try. If theirs were a match that was meant to be, shouldn't all of this have come naturally? Shouldn't their minds have been as perfectly attuned as their bodies obviously were?

When they finally pulled to a stop in her driveway, after the long, silent drive home from the carnival, she glanced over at Tate and found him staring straight ahead. A stormy expression was on his face, and his hands clutched the steering wheel with white-knuckled intensity. She noted idly that he hadn't turned off the engine. It seemed as if he could hardly wait for her to get out of the car before going on.

"Tate," she said softly.

"What?"

"I'm sorry."

"Sure."

"I am, but you know I'm right. You're trying to change. I'm trying to change. In the middle of all this changing, we're going to lose ourselves."

He scowled at her. "I have never asked you to change and, frankly, I haven't seen any signs that you've tried. You're still living with your head in the clouds, expecting everything to be romantic and wonderful without any effort. Sorry, honey, but that's not how it works in real life. People have to work at relationships. If you don't wake up and accept that, you're going to lead a very lonely life. That perfect fairy-tale hero on the white charger is never going to show up."

"I'm not waiting for some guy on a white charger," she huffed indignantly, though she wondered if he might not be right. Jeannie had accused her of the same thing often enough. But even if it were true, was it so terribly wrong to want someone who could capture her imagination and make it fly, who would soar with her through each day and fill it with color and light and laughter?

"Aren't you?" Tate was saying skeptically. "It seems to me you aren't about to be satisfied with some ordinary man who happens to love you. He doesn't wield a lot of flowery phrases or go out slaying dragons on his lunch hour."

"Is that what you think I want?"

"Of course it is. You've made that plain. No matter how hard I tried, I always disappointed you."

"That's not true. I loved you for trying."

"But it was never enough, was it?" he said sadly. "If it had been, some stupid fortune-teller couldn't have thrown you like this. She gave you an excuse to bow out, because my loving you and wanting to protect you and take care of you was never enough. You wanted the moon, and I could only give you the stars."

His words, a paraphrase of those from her favorite movie which they'd watched together a few nights ago, shook Victoria to her very core. What had she done? Did she expect more than any woman had a right to ask of a man? Had she wanted him to do all of the changing, while she sat back and waited until he turned into an appropriate hero who plucked not only stars, but the moon, from the sky for her?

He was staring at her and to her amazement, his eyes were glistening with unshed tears. "Well, I'm tired of trying," he said softly. "Maybe that fortune-teller did us a favor, after all. I finally see that I've been wasting my time."

"Oh, Tate," Victoria whispered, stunned now that it really was all crashing down around them. Somehow she'd expected Tate to argue with her, to fight for the relationship. At the carnival, he'd seemed so angry, so incredulous that she would throw it all away. But in the end apparently he'd also seen the truth of what she'd said. On the long drive home, all of the fight had drained out of him.

"I didn't mean for it to end this way," she said miserably. "I thought for a while we could make it work. I really did."

"So did I," he replied quietly, his gaze locking with hers, holding it, until Victoria felt her breath catch in her throat. "Good night, Victoria."

She hesitated for just a moment, not wanting to open the door of the car, not wanting to take that final step that would finish things between them. She started to say something, but Tate silenced her with a trembling finger held against her quivering lips.

"We've said enough," he said softly.

Victoria sighed and nodded. She got out of the car and closed the door quietly. The sound was more devastatingly final than if she'd slammed it. As Tate backed out of the driveway, she watched him go, hot, sorrowful tears at long last streaming down her cheeks.

"Goodbye," she murmured. When Lancelot wound between her legs, meowing softly, she picked him up and held him so tightly that he howled in protest. "Sorry, old guy," she apologized. "You're all I've got now."

No matter how many times in the next few weeks Victoria told herself that what had happened had been for the best, she was miserable. It might have been the right thing to do in the long run, but in the short run it was absolute hell. She thought continually about Tate's charge that her expectations had been unrealistic. Perhaps she had idealized romance in such a way that no mere human being could ever fulfill her dreams. Ironically, the more she mulled this over, the more she realized that Tate had fulfilled more of her dreams than she'd ever had any right to hope for. He'd been tender and caring and more than willing to tolerate—even indulge—her craziness. To her surprise, he'd even seemed to love her all the more because of it. So what if he'd been allergic to bees. He'd been willing to risk being stung to be with her. The same was true of all the rest of those crazy things they'd done together.

The problem, she finally admitted, hadn't been his acceptance of her at all. It had been her stupid inability to accept him. She had interpreted his dependability as stuffiness, his protectiveness as an attempt to dominate, his down-to-earth realism as an attempt to stifle her creativity. Even though she could see now that she had been the one lacking in imagination in terms of their relationship, she still felt that Tate was better off without her. Their differences ultimately would create strain, not excitement, and nothing anyone could say was likely to change her mind.

Goodness knows everyone had tried hard enough. Her parents were tired of watching her mope around. When her father's subtle, kindly questions drew no response, her mother had sat her down in the kitchen, poured her a cup of tea and demanded answers. When that didn't work, they had sent Jeannie over with strawberry shortcake, whipped cream, advice and sympathy so thick you could practically slice it with a knife. Victoria had eaten the shortcake, ignored the advice, choked on the sympathy and kept her innermost thoughts to herself.

After all of that, however, she did make an attempt to rally. She actually went to a farm sale, but instead of the excitement she usually felt, she became more depressed than ever. Images of Tate bidding wildly on the Fiestaware dishes just to please her teased her mind, taunted her with the realization that she'd had her storybook hero at her side and hadn't even known it.

On the day the envelope from the IRS arrived, Victoria broke down and cried for the first time since the night she and Tate had broken up. She couldn't even bear to open it. She was sitting behind the counter in the front of the shop, sniffling and wiping her eyes with the back of her hand when a woman in her mid-fifties breezed in. She was wearing a bright green jump suit and a colorful flowing scarf around her neck. At the sight of Victoria sobbing all by herself, a frown creased her brow, and the twinkle in her dark brown eyes died.

"Oh, dear," she said, clucking sympathetically. "Have you had bad news? Should I come back another time?"

Victoria waved the letter and shook her head, but she couldn't seem to stop the flow of tears. The woman reached into the huge bag she was carrying and dug around for several minutes. She pulled out a crumbling pack of peanut butter crackers, the nozzle for a garden hose, two paperbacks—one on astrology and another on the history of civilization—and a pair of bifocals before finally extracting a tissue and handing it to Victoria.

"Never can find things when you need them," she muttered under her breath, as Victoria realized with widening eyes that the woman's purse wasn't a handbag at all, but a plastic tote bag from Harrod's in a shade of olive-green that clashed horribly with her outfit. She put her glasses on and took the letter that Victoria had dropped on the counter.

"Do you mind?" she asked, peering over the top of the bifocals.

Victoria shook her head. What did it matter who read it? Either she was going to jail or she wasn't. What the letter really meant was that Tate hated her so much, he hadn't wanted to tell her in person. The woman was staring intently from the envelope to Victoria and back again as though she understood that. Suddenly Victoria forgot about her own pain and began to wonder who on earth this sympathetic, perceptive woman was.

"Who are you?" she asked at last.

"Lisa McAndrews," the woman replied matter-of-factly, as Victoria's pulse began to race.

"McAndrews? Tate's..."

"That's right, dear," she said with a bright smile that made her look like an impish girl. "I'm Tate's mother."

Victoria tried to snatch the letter back. She couldn't have Tate's mother finding out about this whole IRS mess. What on earth would the woman think of her?

"Don't be silly," Mrs. McAndrews said, holding the letter out of her reach. "There's no use your getting all upset over this, when you don't even know what it says."

She gave Victoria a sharp, considering glance. "But that's not what you're upset about anyway, is it?"

Startled, Victoria simply stared at her. "How did you know?"

"I'm a woman. I also know what a bullheaded fool my son can be."

Victoria shook her head miserably. "I'm the one who's been the fool."

"Scattering the blame around isn't going to help a thing, my dear, but if you miss him...." She peered at Victoria over the top of her glasses. "You do miss him, don't you?"

"Terribly."

"Then why don't you do something about it?"

"It's not as simple as that. I really don't think there's any point. We're wrong for each other."

"Do you love him?" Tate's mother asked bluntly.

Victoria hesitated, but saw no reason not to be honest. "Yes."

"And he loves you."

"Did he say that?" Victoria asked hopefully.

"Well," Mrs. McAndrews admitted reluctantly. "Not in so many words."

Victoria sighed in disappointment. "No. He wouldn't."

"But he does. All the signs are there. Those ridiculously healthy plants of his are all dying, for heaven's sakes."

"His plants are dying?" Victoria's eyes lit up with a tiny glimmer of renewed hope. She couldn't have been happier if he'd sent her roses.

"And he came over after work the other day, and I noticed that his socks didn't match."

"His socks didn't match?" Her spirits began to skyrocket.

Lisa McAndrews chuckled. "I think you're beginning to catch on. The man's a basket case. If you don't do something about it soon, my sensible son is likely to quit his job and go hang out on a beach with a surfboard."

The very idea boggled Victoria's mind. "You're not serious?"

"Well," she said with a grin, "Perhaps that is a bit of an exaggeration, but he is at the end of his rope. Pete Harrison called me the other day and asked me if I thought Tate was under too much stress."

"Why on earth would his boss ask that?"

"He'd just turned down a complicated case that a few months ago he would have killed to get. He told

Pete he was bored with the corporate cases. Needless to say, Pete was in a state of shock. Fortunately, he didn't guess that Tate's state of mind had anything to do with you, or your audit would have been held up for months while he went over it with a fine-tooth comb.''

"How do you know that's not what he did anyway?"

"Come to think of it, you're right." She ripped open the envelope before Victoria could stop her. "Nope. You're in the clear. The government even apologizes for putting you to so much trouble." She clucked and her brows lifted. "And well they should. Anyone with half a brain can see that you're no criminal. That son of mine must have had a screw loose when he came down here and accused you of who-knows-what."

"He was just doing his job," Victoria defended.

"Frankly, I've always thought it was a lousy job. He'd be much better off if he found something with a little life to it. All those deadly little numbers, lined up in neat little rows...." Her voice trailed off, and she shuddered dramatically. "It gives me the chills."

"I know what you mean."

"Then save him from it," Mrs. McAndrews urged.

Victoria sighed. "I'm not sure we can make it work."

"You love each other," she reminded her simply. "After that, very little else matters."

"But we're so unsuitable."

"By whose standards? Certainly not mine. I led my husband on a merry chase, let me tell you. I think that's why Tate started out being so cautious with you. He was always convinced that his father and I were totally unsuited.''

"I'm sure he didn't really believe that,'' Victoria said.

"Oh, yes, he did. I heard him say it to his father often enough, when he thought I wasn't listening.''

"That's awful.''

"No, it wasn't. Not really. He was just being protective. He was worried that my antics were going to drive his father over the edge.'' She grinned impishly. "Actually, we were a perfect match. I brought a lot of fun and craziness into his life, and he kept me out of jail. We were very much in love. I think you and Tate are, too. You can work it out.

"And just think,'' she added with a conspiratorial smile, "You'll never have to worry about balancing your checkbook again.''

"Since you know about the audit, then you know I've never worried about that anyway,'' Victoria replied wryly. "Much to your son's dismay.''

Lisa McAndrews threw her arms around Victoria and hugged her impulsively. "Go to him, my dear. I've always wanted a daughter-in-law just like you. We will have the most wonderful time.''

They would, too, Victoria thought. She knew instinctively that she and Tate's mother were two of a kind, just as he was the son-in-law her parents had always dreamed of. That ought to count for something. Maybe this whole thing wasn't quite so crazy after all.

She gave Lisa McAndrews a dazzling smile.

"You're going to do it, aren't you?" the older woman said, her brown eyes twinkling just as Victoria had seen Tate's do on those occasions when she did something to delight him.

"I'm going to think about it."

"Don't think, dear. That's what got you in trouble in the first place. Listen to your heart," she advised, as she gathered her things and breezed out.

When she had gone, Victoria listened as hard as she could. Her heart was soaring.

Twelve

———

Tate stood in front of the steamed up bathroom mirror and took a good hard look at himself. Even through the foggy distortion, the image was enough to make him shudder. Today was his thirtieth birthday, and he looked like a man who'd been on a nonstop, three-week bender, and he hadn't even taken a drink. Not that he hadn't wanted to. Every time an image of Victoria had popped into his mind, he'd wanted to dull it with alcohol, but he'd forced himself to live with the vivid, beguiling impressions. They had dominated his days and taunted him in his dreams.

When Pete had told him to send the letter telling Victoria that the audit was complete and that there'd been no evidence of fraud or tax evasion, he'd thought that would be the end of it. He'd replace her case with another, her image with that of a new woman. Instead, the cases had bored him, and every woman he'd called had sounded so ridiculously sophisticated, so disgustingly normal and uninteresting, he'd hung up without ever asking for a date. He'd spent his evenings alone with his memories. Crazy, wacky, wonderful memories of the unexpected that always seemed to happen whenever Victoria was involved.

There would be no more of that, he solemnly told his reflection. His birthday was as good a day as any to start over, to get himself back on track again. Maybe he'd even quit his job and leave Cincinnati, check out new options and new horizons. The old ones had left him feeling increasingly dissatisfied ever since Victoria had opened his eyes to new possibilities.

An hour later he was sitting in his office trying to work up the courage to tell Pete he wanted to quit or, at the very least, transfer to another IRS office, when he heard a chorus of laughter floating through the outer offices. He opened the door and peered out to see what had brought on this totally unexpected, raucous sound. Pete frowned on joviality. In fact, right now Pete was standing outside his office, shaking his head and muttering dire curses under his breath.

"What's going on?" Tate asked.

"You tell me, McAndrews," he groused.

"What's that supposed to mean?"

"I think you'd better go check out the elevator."

"The elevator?" His head started spinning in that same crazy, light-headed way it always had when Victoria was up to something. It hadn't happened to him in weeks now.

He walked through the main office, noticing that everyone seemed to be either studiously ignoring him or grinning like the proverbial cat who'd just lunched on a very satisfying canary. When he reached the elevator, he began to understand why. The door was lodged open by a clown wearing a puffy, polka-dotted costume, a bright-orange fright wig and oversized shoes. One foot was propped against the left door, while the clown's very attractive rear poked against the right door. Both hands were frantically trying to pull a tangled bunch of helium-filled balloons through the doors before they smashed shut.

Tate started to chuckle at the perfectly incongruous sight, but the sound died in his throat as one of the balloons floated close enough for him to get a good look at it. He groaned softly and closed his eyes, hoping that when he opened them again, he'd discover that he'd only imagined that every one of the red, silver and blue balloons said "Happy Birthday, Tate" in bright green lettering. He peeked again. Nothing had changed. Without even counting, he knew there would be thirty balloons in that elevator. He prayed innocent, claustrophobic people weren't stuck in there with them.

His eyes squinted suspiciously and roved over the clown again, and his heart suddenly tripped a little faster. That rear end, poked out so provocatively, looked very familiar despite the baggy costume. Surely it couldn't be....

The clown offered him a lopsided grin. "Are you this Tate person?" an unfamiliar, squeaky little voice asked, throwing him. He stared at the clown more

closely, his brow creasing in a puzzled frown. For a
minute, he'd been so sure, but maybe his mind was
playing tricks on him after all. He'd missed Victoria so
much, his imagination had probably simply conjured
her up for him. The clown, however, was very real and
was waiting for an answer.

"I'm Tate," he admitted reluctantly.

"Sorry about the entrance," the clown squeaked.
"But I'm a little new at this. If you could hold some
of these?"

"Umm...of course," he said, blushing furiously as
the new, unrestrained chuckles started again behind
him. When he had all thirty balloons safely in tow, the
clown released the elevator door and it slowly glided
shut. The clown was inside. Tate was outside, staring
at the elevator in confusion. A minute later, the door
opened revealing an obviously embarrassed clown.

"Sorry. I was supposed to sing."

The clown cleared its throat and began a lusty, only
slightly off-key rendition of "Happy Birthday to
You." The entire office joined in, singing so loudly
that Tate, for the life of him, couldn't be sure if it was
Victoria's sweetly melodious voice he heard or not.
Before he could make a grab for the clown and take a
good hard look into those dancing, seemingly familiar blue eyes, the doors were shut again and the clown
was gone.

"Do you suppose we could get some work done
around here now?" Pete growled next to him, though
there was a decided twinkle in his eyes.

Suddenly, Tate made a decision. He grinned at Pete,
put the strings of the balloons into his hands and

hopped on the next elevator. He thought if he lived to be a hundred, he would never forget the startled grin that had creased Pete's face, right before he'd resumed his more characteristic scowl.

When he reached the lobby, Tate wasn't sure exactly what he was going to do next. He only knew that he had to find that clown—Victoria, he was absolutely sure of it—and make things right between them somehow. As ridiculous as their relationship might be, their fight had been even more absurd. They loved each other, and two reasonably intelligent people should never have been separated by a fortune-teller and a deck of cards. Rational people in love could work things out, cards or no cards. Surely they could find a way to have both balloons and order in their lives.

He drove north as though he'd been sent to put out a raging fire, which, in a manner of speaking, he had. There had been a fire burning inside him for weeks now, and only Victoria had the power to quench the flames. He headed straight for Victoria's shop and found her mother chatting happily with a customer over coffee and cherry pie. He wondered briefly if the crust was soggy or if Victoria had finally mastered crusts.

Katherine Marshall glanced up at his entrance and beamed at him.

"It's about time," she chided gently.

"Where is she?"

"Have you tried the house? She seems to be hiding out there a lot lately."

"I'll have her back here by tomorrow," he promised.

"I'd rather you took her off on a long honeymoon."

He grinned. "I think that can be arranged, too."

When he got to the house, the battered blue Volkswagen was in the driveway. Feeling like an amateur detective, he walked over and laid his hand over the engine. It was still warm. She'd either been to the supermarket, or she'd been to Cincinnati. He was willing to lay odds on Cincinnati.

He knocked on the back door and marched in without even waiting for a response. He took the stairs two at a time. When he reached the top, he hesitated at the closed bathroom door, then shrugged, muttered under his breath and threw it open. Startled blue eyes flew up and met his in the mirror. Golden-red curls tumbled over her shoulders, which were still encased in an oversized clown's costume. He grinned. Her reflection grinned back at him hesitantly.

"You knew, didn't you?"

"Of course, I knew," he said confidently, as if he'd never had a second's doubt. "How many people do you think I know who'd get trapped in an elevator with thirty balloons?"

"Two that I can think of."

He chuckled. "You've met my mother."

Victoria nodded.

"I wondered how long it would take her to get to you."

Victoria knew that she would be forever grateful to Lisa McAndrews for making her see that she and Tate shared all of the important values: love, respect, family loyalty. They just expressed them differently. She did wildly impulsive things for those she cared about. Tate expressed his caring in a more sedate manner, but the sentiment was just as strong, just as real.

"She was worried about you," she told Tate now.

"And you?"

"I was too busy being miserable and confused and mad at myself to worry about you."

"Me, too," he admitted. "I was being miserable and stubborn."

Victoria gave him a dimpled smile, that was emphasized by the rosy-red greasepaint on her cheeks. "You're very good at stubborn."

"You're not so bad yourself."

She turned around finally and took a step toward him, tilting her head to one side as she studied the face that she had missed so much. She reached out a finger and gently touched the dark circles under his eyes.

"My fault?"

"Nope. Mine."

She nodded. "Your mother says it doesn't matter whose fault it is, as long as we work it out."

"Wise woman, my mother."

Victoria grinned. "You might tell her that sometime. She's convinced you think she's a flake.

"She is."

"Tate!"

"That doesn't mean I don't love her, just like it doesn't mean I can't love you. It just took me a while to figure that out."

"Wise man," Victoria noted, gazing into his eyes, her heart warming at the answers she saw there, answers to all of her unasked questions. She grinned at him impishly.

"Did you like the balloons?"

Golden lights danced in his eyes. "I don't suppose you could have sent a card?"

She shook her head. "Boring. Would you have driven up here after me if you'd gotten some dumb old card in the mail?"

"Probably," he admitted. "But Pete wouldn't have had nearly as much fun."

"Pete?"

"I left the balloons with him."

"He must have loved that."

"Actually I think he did. You may be saving two men from boredom, instead of only one."

"I've always believed in getting a good deal."

"Since when?"

"Since I fell in love with a man who's keeping a close watch on my finances."

"Is that all you're interested in? My financial skills?"

She took another step closer and circled her arms around his neck. "Well, there is this other little skill I've noticed...."

"What's that?" he teased.

"Let me show you." Her lips brushed across his lightly, then returned with a firmer, hungrier touch. When his mouth opened and her tongue flicked across his teeth, she heard a moan rumble deep in his throat, and his arms tightened around her.

"Don't you ever leave me again," he whispered hoarsely. "I don't think I could stand it."

"There is one way to be sure I won't," she taunted, grinning at him impishly.

"What's that?"

"If I have to tell you, it doesn't count."

"Oh," he said. "That way."

She nodded, as Tate dropped dramatically to one knee.

"Victoria Marshall, will you marry me?" he asked solemnly.

She studied him considerably. "That's an awfully traditional proposal."

"Too traditional?" he teased, his brown eyes twinkling in the way that always made her feel as if he'd earned a Nobel prize.

"Much. I was thinking along the lines of a skywriter."

"Okay," he said agreeably. "Tell me where I can hire one."

"You'd really do that for me?"

"I would do almost anything for you. Don't you know that by now?" he asked as the phone rang. He groaned. "Not again."

"Hush," Victoria soothed. "I'll get rid of them."

She picked up the phone and talked briefly, her lips curving into a smile. "I'll tell him," she promised.

"Tell me what? Who was that?"

"It was your mother."

"How did she know I was here?"

"She said she knew it was only a matter of time."

"What did she want?"

"She had this great idea for our honeymoon."

"*She* had a great idea for *our* honeymoon? What made her think we were getting married?"

"She said that was only a matter of time, too."

Tate moaned. "Good Lord. What am I doing to myself? I'll never be able to cope with the two of you."

"Don't worry," Victoria consoled him. "You'll have my parents on your side."

"That may help some. What exactly did my mother have in mind for our honeymoon?"

"She wanted us to go on an archaeological dig."

"What?"

"With her."

"Victoria!"

"I think it would be fun."

"No. Uh-uh. Absolutely not. That would not be a honeymoon."

"Who says?"

Tate sighed. "Victoria do you know anything at all about archaeology?"

"No. Do you?"

"No."

"Then that's all the more reason for us to go."

"Victoria, I may not know much about digs, but I know a little about honeymoons. Mothers do not go."

"Who says? Miss Manners?"

"No. I do."

"Spoilsport."

Tate sighed. "How about if we go on our honeymoon alone and then go on an archaeological dig with my mother?"

"Oh, okay," she agreed finally. "I guess that makes sense."

"Thank goodness. Since you're so anxious to plan the honeymoon, does that mean you're accepting my proposal?"

"Oh," she said innocently, "Didn't I give you an answer?"

"You did not. Am I going to have to wait to see if I pass some other test?"

"Oh, you've passed all the tests," she said softly. "With flying colors."

"Hallelujah!" he said fervently. "Then you won't mind helping me up."

"Can't you get up?"

"No. I seem to have thrown my back out."

"Oh, Tate, not again."

"Again," he confirmed. "But it's okay. I'm getting used to it."

"Want me to kiss it and make it better?" she offered hopefully.

Tate regarded her skeptically. "Do you actually think that will work?"

"It's worth a try," she said, smiling at him suggestively.

"Now that you mention...."

Her delicate touch skimmed over him and suddenly his back did feel better. In fact his entire body felt as if it were floating on air. "Not bad, Victoria. Keep it up."

"I plan to," she promised. "For a lifetime."

Silhouette Desire

**Available
January 1987**

NEVADA
SILVER

The third book in the exciting
Desire Trilogy by Joan Hohl.

The Sharp brothers are back, along with
sister Kit ... and Logan McKittrick.

Kit's loved Logan all her life and, with a little
help from the silver glow of a Nevada night,
she must convince the stubborn rancher that
she's a woman who needs a man's love—not
the protection of another brother.

Don't miss *Nevada Silver*—Kit and
Logan's story and the conclusion
of Joan Hohl's acclaimed
Desire Trilogy.

DT-C-1

FOUR UNIQUE SERIES
FOR EVERY WOMAN YOU ARE..

Silhouette Romance

Heartwarming romances that will make you
laugh and cry as they bring you all the wonder
and magic of falling in love.

6 titles
per month

Silhouette Special Edition

Expanded romances written with emotion and
heightened romantic tension to ensure
powerful stories. A rare blend of passion and
dramatic realism.

6 titles
per month

Silhouette Desire

Believable, sensuous, compelling—and
above all, romantic—these stories deliver
the promise of love, the guarantee
of satisfaction.

6 titles
per month

Silhouette Intimate Moments

Love stories that entice; longer, more
sensuous romances filled with adventure,
suspense, glamour and melodrama.

4 titles
per month

Silhouette Romances
not available in retail outlets in Canada